AND THEN THEY DIE

AND THEN THEY DIE

Robert McCollum

A
Joan
Kahn
BOOK

St. Martin's Press
New York

Design by Paolo Pepe

Library of Congress Cataloging in Publication Data

McCollum, Robert.
  And then they die.
  "A Joan Kahn book"

  I. Title.
PS3563.C3433A83   1985   813'.54   84-22870
ISBN 0-312-03615-9

First Edition

10 9 8 7 6 5 4 3 2 1

To Judy

. . . Most men eddy about
Here and there, eat and drink,
Chatter and love and hate,
Gather and squander, are raised
Aloft, are hurled in the dust,
Striving blindly, achieving
Nothing; and then they die . . .
       —Matthew Arnold
        from "Rugby Chapel"

AND THEN THEY DIE

1

THERE was no moon, and the outside lights were not working; however, as Claudine Taylor peered out the window of her second-story bedroom, she was certain she could make out a slowly moving shadow near the shrubbery to the left of the swimming pool. Whatever was casting the shadow was hidden by the bushes and the low hedge and by the angle of the main house itself.

Moments earlier Claudine had heard the dogs barking and had risen to see if she could determine what was upsetting them. There had been red wolf and coyote hybrids about lately, out of the pine forests, running in packs; and their scent had probably been picked up by the caged Dobermans. She knew that for safety's sake she should have opened their cage and let them roam freely on the grounds. But with the servants off on their annual two-week vacation it would have meant that she would have to round up the dogs herself in the morning; and at her age that was no simple task. The last time she had tried it, it had taken all morning, and by the time she had the last dog caged, she had been thoroughly exhausted.

But now, as she watched the moving shadow glide closer to the house, she wished desperately that she had let the dogs out. They would have cut down any intruder—animal or human.

Surely the shape in the bushes was a coyote or some other night animal. But the shadow seemed too long. Still, the night can play tricks on one's eyes—especially if the eyes are sixty-five years old and were none too strong forty years ago.

The shadow grew more distinct. Where was the background light coming from? No moon, no stars, no outside lights. She shifted her gaze upward. The moon must be straining behind the thick clouds and forcing some light around their dark edges. And even though the inside lights were all turned off, the house itself must be radiating heat and light.

Claudine lowered her eyes once again to the shrubbery. But the angle was wrong now, and the shadow had dissolved behind the corner of the morning room.

In an instinctive gesture she gathered her nightgown closer to her neck. She made a quick decision. She was being silly, she knew, but better safe than sorry. She crossed the room swiftly and reached for the telephone beside her bed. It rang six long, slow times before it was answered, and even then she had to speak first.

"Hello, hello!"

"Kilkenny Police Station," a sleepy voice finally responded. "Officer Ridgeway."

"This is Claudine Taylor at Fairfield! I may have an intruder out here!"

The voice leapt to attention. "Mrs. Taylor! Yes, ma'am! An intruder—have you seen him?"

"No, I'm not sure. But can you send someone?"

"Of course, right away. I'm sure there's a car on the highway. I'll get on the radio. It won't be long."

"Thank you." She replaced the receiver.

She returned to the window and looked toward the corner of the morning room to see if the shadow might have reformed to begin moving in the opposite direction, away from the house. But there was nothing to be seen. And all along the hedge and beside the shrubs, there was only the dark grass.

She stood very still and listened carefully. She tried to remember if she had locked all of the downstairs doors and windows. It was not part of her normal nightly routine, since the servants generally secured the house for the night, but she was certain she had taken the proper care. She made a silent vow never again to allow the servants all to leave at the same time. It had seemed such a simple, organized way to handle their vacations; but now it seemed incredibly foolish.

The dogs had quieted down. Did that mean that the intruder had left the grounds, or was he inside the house? Or had the whole thing been the result of an old woman's morbid imagination?

She turned from the window and stared toward the door of her bedroom. She was glad she had left it open. The sight of a slowly turning doorknob might be more than a weak heart could bear.

And now another breach in her security struck her. A household dog—even a nervous little poodle—would have told her if someone was inside. She made another vow. In the morning she would drive to Dallas and find the most anxious, fidgety little house dog available—one that would bark and yap at everyone . . . even the children when they came to visit. She didn't wish to go through this again.

A stairboard creaked. And then another. She gasped and with her left hand drew her nightgown even tighter to her throat. Irrationally, she wished she had on a robe. She thought about crossing to the closet on the far side of the room to get one, but she was too terrified to move.

Another creak, and another. And then no sound whatever.

Where were the police? Why weren't they hurrying? Then she realized it had been only a few seconds since she called; and even if a cruiser were close to the highway intersection, it was at least twenty minutes more down the side roads to Fairfield.

There were no additional sounds. The stairs and the hallway were silent. She crossed herself and ventured a tentative step, and then stopped to listen once again. Nothing. She moved forward, this time taking two steps; she stopped again and remained still for a full minute—perhaps two, she couldn't be sure. No sound. She began to breathe more regularly. Dogs barking, shadows outside, stairs creaking. She smiled at her excitability. A counterfeit crisis.

She walked swiftly forward now to verify her new confidence. The blackness beyond the doorway almost caused her to stop again, but she shrugged and burst through as if to say, see there—a counterfeit!

But once in the hallway she knew instantly she'd been wrong. She sensed another presence in the darkness—behind her. She began to turn slowly, to confront the trespasser who had caused her so much trouble. She was not afraid. She would see just what this was all about. But when she had done a complete about-face, she felt the full force of her fear return. There was nothing there. She had been wrong about another presence. She looked back toward the stairs. Terror mixed with confusion.

And then the dark shape, which had been crouching low in the blackness and which she had overlooked, rose up behind her and grabbed her by the hair, twisting and jerking her head violently until her thin neck popped, once, twice—sending odd echoes down the dark stairs. She died instantly, without another thought. But as she lay on her back on the hardwood floor, her head at a crazy angle, the intruder knelt beside her. He pulled a long curved knife from his belt and plunged it deep into her right shoulder. He then yanked it free and drove it into her left shoulder— twisting, twisting, twisting.

He left the knife in place and sprang quickly to his feet. He sensed that his time was limited. She had obviously detected his approach, since she had crept so carefully across her bedroom and into the hall. That might mean that she had called for help. If so there was no time to lose. Ten minutes at the most, and he must be gone.

From his shirt pocket he withdrew a small slip of paper. He went straight to the bedroom closet and threw open the door. He entered, closed the door behind him, and turned on the light. The massive safe stood like a fortress at the far end of the closet.

2

*I have taken carbolic acid, and may God have
mercy on my poor soul.*

FRANCESCA Mills continued to stare at the short suicide note. Carbolic acid. My God, couldn't the old lady have used sleeping pills or something? Carbolic acid! How hideous—and how old-fashioned, for that matter. Frankie reproached herself for being so cynical. Surely when the old lady lay down to die, she was not concerned with what was fashionable. Carbolic acid it was.

Without a doubt it was a front-page story. Hell, Beta Lan Franco's garden parties were front-page stories in the *Kilkenny Weekly Times*. But how should it be set up? Headlines? No, too macabre; and anyway there was the bond election. The local yokels would want to know how that turned out. School playgrounds no less. Didn't they care about the Middle East . . . Washington? She shook her head. But that's not really fair, she thought. They had television; and they could always pick up the *Dallas Times-Herald* or the *Morning News.* They didn't need her pitiful rag for world and national news. So the bond election it was . . . and the death of old Mrs. Erikson. Poor soul. Poor soul indeed.

Maybe a side bar beneath the election results: FORMER KILKENNY RESIDENT COMES HOME TO DIE. Yes, that was just right. She adjusted her typewriter, typed the heading, and began to compose the first few lines of the story.

Karen Erikson, former resident of Kilkenny, Texas, came home Friday—apparently for the first time in over forty years. But her visit did not last long. After checking into the Ramada Inn Friday evening and pursuing private memories for a day and a half, she decided to take her own life. She was found Sunday afternoon, fully clothed, on her bed at the hotel. There was no indication of foul play. In a concise suicide note, which was found lying beside her on the bed, she explained that she had taken carbolic acid, and invoked the mercies of the Almighty. Gregg County Precinct Judge, Susan Moreno, has not yet decided on the disposition of the body. She has two choices: assign a local doctor to do the autopsy, or ship the remains to Dallas where the resources of the Dallas County Medical Examiner's Office will be . . .

She stopped in mid-sentence, removed her fingers from the keys, and stared at the page. Maybe she was selling this story short. Who was this old girl, Karen Erikson, anyway? Why did she come home to die? Where had she been for the last forty years? And what had she done between Friday night and Sunday morning?

She looked at the suicide note again. When she'd borrowed it from Police Chief Boone she'd toyed with the idea of reproducing it (torn edges and all) on the front page, next to the story. But twenty years with *The New York Times* had bred in her a reserve that made such a garish display repugnant. She would not change her style just because the only newspaper she had been able to afford was located in a small town in East Texas. Let the rustics upgrade their reading habits. Tomorrow's edition of the *Kilkenny Weekly Times* would carry a description of the note, nothing more. She might be the owner of a rag, but, by God, it would be a dignified rag.

And it would be written with care and diligence, she thought, realizing that all of the information on the Karen Erikson story had come to her secondhand. Chief Boone had told her about the hotel, Judge Moreno—everything. She hadn't taken the time to interview anyone. If she had turned in such a story in New York, she'd have been out on her ass on Forty-third Street, looking for a job, before her type-writer cooled down. Reporters are not supposed to parrot what they're told by authorities. They're supposed to dig out the information for themselves. And anyway, what the hell kind of authority was Chief Boone in the first place— the goddamned ignorant hayseed. The man was a hick— born and raised—and here she was using him as her sole source for a news story. She should be defrocked. And to make matters worse, she was reasonably certain that the beer-bellied son of a bitch was grunting romantic noises in her direction.

She looked up to see that her printer, Gabriel Sullivan, had walked into the room. He was coming from the press room and his apron was soaked in ink; however, it was im-possible to tell if he'd been at the presses, since he was al-ways covered in ink no matter what tasks he'd been performing. Even his sparse gray hair was laced with dark blue streaks. He sat down heavily on the edge of Frankie's desk.

"Front page done?" he asked.

"Not yet, Gabe. I've been working on this story on Karen Erikson's suicide."

Sullivan nodded. "Sad thing."

"Did you know her, Gabe? You're about her age, I think."

"A little older. Karen must have been twenty-two or so when she took off. That'd make her . . . let's see, sixty-two. I'm sixty-seven, Mrs. Mills. But I told you the truth when you bought the paper last year. Sixty-six, I said. No sense lying." His voice had grown nervous.

"Relax, Gabe. I'm not going to retire you. You can work

here until you're ninety if you're up to it. Just tell me about Karen Erikson."

"I didn't really know her. I knew her husband Samuel a little—used to do some work for him. But I didn't know him good. They was rich, you know. The Eriksons was the richest in town."

Frankie looked at her watch. Two-thirty. The paper was due on the street at 7:00 A.M.—a little over four hours. No chance to interview anyone at this hour. And she couldn't use what Gabe was telling her either—no corroboration. The years could have clouded his memory. She'd have to talk to several sources to verify everything. She'd have to go with the short blurb she'd been writing. The meat of the story would have to wait until next Monday's edition.

"Gabe, I'd like to talk to you some more about Karen Erikson. Maybe tomorrow after the paper's out. But now we'd better get busy. I'll have the front page for you in fifteen minutes."

Sullivan nodded and returned to the press room, rubbing an ink-stained hand across the back of his neck.

After her printer disappeared, Frankie finished composing the article on the Erikson suicide, and then laid out the rest of the front page (with heavy emphasis on the bond election). She was about to call out to Sullivan to tell him that it was time to set up, when she felt an unpleasant but familiar heavy sensation on the lower right side of her body. She dropped her right hand for confirmation, and then rose and walked quickly across the room toward the small restroom off the workshop. As she walked, she thought of Police Chief Garner "Blackie" Boone, and she wondered what kind of romantic inclinations the coarse bastard would have if he knew the truth about her.

When she returned from her ablutions, she was drawn and subdued. Her eyes were red and dark, and her breathing labored and irregular. She stood beside her desk for some moments before lowering her thin, long-boned frame into her chair.

She found it difficult to resume her concentration, but before long she shrugged and leaned forward. She reexamined the work she had done previously, and then called for Sullivan. He responded promptly, appearing at the connecting door in a matter of seconds.

"Gabe, the front page is finished," she said softly.

Before the old man could answer, there was an insistent rapping on the glass outer door.

Frankie glanced at her watch. "Three A.M. What the hell? It must be someone from that damned security outfit—letting us know they come around once in awhile."

But as she approached the door, she could see the large round face of Police Chief Boone staring through the glass. She opened the door and said, "Chief Boone, come in. Is this a social call? A bit late, isn't it?" She left him standing in the open doorway and walked back toward her desk.

"No, not a social call," he said, trotting after her. "But please call me Blackie. Chief Boone sounds so formal. And we've known each other over a year now, Frankie."

"Hello, Blackie," Gabriel Sullivan said, walking toward them.

"Hey, Gabe, how's it going?"

Frankie frowned. "What is it you need, Blackie? I've got a newspaper to get out. More about Karen Erikson's suicide?"

"No, I'm afraid not," he replied slowly. "We've got a murder on our hands. Claudine Taylor out at Fairfield. Looks like a burglar. Thought you'd like to hear about it before the paper comes out."

"Good God! When?"

"Just got back. Looks like she was killed a little after eleven."

"Does the congressman know? And her other children?"

"Only Greg. Hard case. Took the news like he was getting the score on the Cowboys' game. Congressman Taylor's supposed to be in Longview, but I couldn't locate him there. As for Winnie, who the hell knows? She could be anywhere around here—if you know what I mean? No answer at her place, and the boys I sent over there tell me it's locked up tighter than a nun's . . . locked up tight. Winnie's not known for sleeping in her own bed. She—"

Frankie interrupted him. "How was Claudine Taylor killed?"

"Broken neck. Stabbed. We'll need a good autopsy on this one. Judge Moreno's already out there. I'm sure she'll send the body to Dallas."

"A burglar you say?"

"Looks like it. The safe in her bedroom closet was standing wide open. A piece of paper with the combination written on it was lying on top of the safe. Looks like he forced it out of her before he killed her. We'll probably find he tortured her with the knife. One thing though. The guy wasn't satisfied with what he found in the safe. The drawers and cupboards all over the house were ransacked. The place's a mess."

She asked thoughtfully, "What else do we know so far?"

For the next few minutes, while Frankie took precise notes, the cooperative police chief explained about Claudine Taylor's call for help, the annual servants' vacation, the caged Doberman pinschers, and all of the other important aspects of the case. It was his belief, he said, that the citizens should know as much of the truth as possible, as quickly as possible, so that false and unhelpful rumors would not spread.

When Chief Boone had gone, Frankie looked up at the mock-up of the front page that she had done earlier. She pushed it aside and said to Gabriel Sullivan, "We'll have to work fast!"

He nodded but said nothing.

She paused for a minute and considered her repugnance toward sensationalism. Dignity and decorum were certainly important. Opinions and ideas and news stories of substance and significance were the hallmarks of any respectable newspaper. Then she thought, to hell with it! This is not New York, and this is certainly not *The New York Times.* She quickly blocked out a bold forty-eight-point headline to run across the top of the front page that read: SUICIDE AT THE RAMADA INN; and below that in a very black seventy-two-point headline: CLAUDINE TAYLOR BRUTALLY MURDERED. She re-read the Karen Erikson story and decided it was okay as written. She laid it in at the left top of the page with a small subheadline declaring: FORMER RESIDENT COMES HOME TO DIE. Next she began writing the Taylor murder story, which she would place slightly lower and to the right, but with a larger subheadline, and with twice the column space.

She began:

> Suicide is rare in Kilkenny, Texas, but murder is
> very rare indeed. . . .

3

A N hour later Frankie sat in Blackie Boone's office at City Hall watching a steady stream of Kilkenny's leading citizens march in and out, shaking their sleepy heads in dismay over the tragedy in their midst. Most either totally ignored her or gave her a cursory nod. She knew that they considered her an outsider, a pushy New Yorker, severe, uppity, aggressive. East Texas businessmen were a clannish lot. Assertive transplants (especially women) ranked very low on their totem of mutual back scratchers. She had heard that a good number of local merchants were considering dropping the *Kilkenny Weekly Times* altogether, even if it was the only newspaper in town. Goddamn their syrupy Southern manners and their devious hearts.

Her thoughts were interrupted by Officer Bobby Ridgeway, who leaned his head around the door to Chief Boone's office.

"Chief, we finally tracked down Congressman Taylor. He's in Longview—at Edgar Brooks's place. We haven't told him anything. He's on the phone. Line two."

"Thanks, Bobby," Blackie said. His face darkened, and Frankie could see that he was very reluctant to take the call.

"Hello, Jake. Blackie Boone. I'm afraid there's terrible news here in Kilkenny! . . . It's your mother. She's been murdered. . . . Out at Fairfield. Looks like an intruder. . . . We've notified Greg. He's on his way. We haven't found Winnie yet. I'm sure we'll turn her up soon. Jake, could you come right away? There's a lot we need. . . . No, nothing yet on who did it. . . . Yes, Jake, terrible."

He hung up the telephone, and said to Frankie, "Nasty business. The one part of this job I'll never get used to."

"Where's he been?" she asked.

"Out talking politics. This Senate race, you know."

A few seconds later Officer Ridgeway stuck his head around the door once again. It was obvious that he had been waiting for the telephone extension light to go out.

Blackie said, "Come on in, Bobby. Don't stand out in the hall like a stepchild."

Bobby Ridgeway nodded, and then inched his tall, slim body around the door very slowly and very reluctantly, as if the chief's office were a sanctum off limits to ordinary mortals.

Frankie watched him, amused. The young policeman took the better part of half a minute to complete his passage through the door, all the while rolling his shoulders and jerking his long neck up and down.

"Sit down, Bobby," Blackie said. "What's on your mind?"

"I need to talk to you for a few minutes, Chief." He sat down on the battered couch next to Frankie, and spent some time tangling and untangling his legs.

Blackie said, "Long night, eh? Claudine Taylor! God, what a mess!"

Ridgeway looked uncomfortably toward Frankie. "I hoped we might talk alone."

"Don't worry about Frankie," said Blackie. "She's going to be part of the family . . . here in Kilkenny. Speak up."

Frankie felt uncomfortable herself, and definitely *not* a part of the Kilkenny family, but she smiled reassuringly and tried to appear motherly.

The young man shrugged and said, "Chief, you've worked nights a lot. Nothing much happens around here at night—unless there's an accident or some kids getting into trouble with booze or grass or just to have something to do. Well, I slept all day, but I was still sleepy before all this started. I might've drifted off once or twice. You know how it is around here at night." His voice trailed off and Frankie thought that the young officer was on the verge of tears.

"Bobby," said Blackie impatiently, "what is it?"

"Chief . . . I *know* I was sleeping earlier. It's not a question of *might've* drifted off. I was sleeping, period! And I didn't even need it. I slept all day—ten, eleven hours." He stared at his feet as he spoke. Then he turned to Blackie, looked him directly in the eyes and said dramatically, "Chief, what if Claudine Taylor tried to call us before? I think I heard the phone ring—somewhere in the back of my mind. I don't think I answered it that time. I'm not sure, but I think I just let it ring. Later when I did answer, I sent Charlie out there. But what if she'd been trying to call and I didn't answer because I was asleep. We might've got there in time. Maybe she died because I'm lazy!"

Blackie said carefully, "Son, did she say anything about calling earlier?"

Ridgeway shook his head.

"Then we'll probably never know who was calling before—*if* someone did call. That's a pretty loud phone out there. You would've gotten it if it really had rung. There's what—three or four calls every night? You could've just imagined that it rang earlier—remembered it from another time."

Ridgeway nodded, but it was obvious that he was not satisfied.

Frankie stared at the nervous young officer and thought that in the future there would be no one more vigilant on the Kilkenny police force.

"Don't think about it anymore, son," Blackie said. "It won't do any good. It's over and done with."

Their somber mood was broken by the turbulent entrance of Officer Charlie Swicegood. Swicegood in no way shared Ridgeway's reluctance to intrude on the boss. He burst into the room like a great black Zulu prince, tossed his hat on Chief Boone's desk, and stood, legs spread, as if he were about to issue marching orders.

"Not a damned thing on Winnie Taylor!" he said, breathing deeply. "Can't find her anywhere. Guess we'll have to wait until morning. She'll come stragglin' in sometime, either to her place or over to the Ramada Inn where she eats breakfast."

Blackie began, "Did you try—"

Swicegood cut his superior off with a sneer as if to say: We tried every place; don't tell me how to do my job!

Blackie said, "In the morning then. It's a shame. We should tell her as soon as possible."

"I got James Lan Franco out there in the waiting room," Swicegood said. "I already told him. He's fuming. He's ready for a lynch mob. But he's got a lot of liquor in him—I think it's just liquor; nowadays even these old guys are mixing dope and booze."

Frankie and the three men left the office and walked through the main room toward the small receiving area near the front door. Officer Ridgeway peeked in to nod at James Lan Franco and then retired to his desk and the phone.

"Hello, James," said Blackie. "Terrible about your sister."

"I want the son of a bitch that did this!" Lan Franco said, rising. He stood with his hands on his hips, his thumbs tucked under his wide leather belt. He was a tall, powerful man, well into his seventies, but still handsome and vital. His wavy silver hair flowed smoothly across his giant skull. Frankie thought as she watched him that for all the world he was the archetypal Texas oilman: violent, arrogant, potent. Even the beet red face was typical, though she was having a difficult time determining whether the color was induced by fury or alcohol.

"It's past five, James," Blackie said, looking at his watch.

Lan Franco's eyes flashed and he snapped, "Sure it's late, and sure I've had a few! Had 'em while Charlie waited for me. Hell, he woke me up to tell me my little sister's been murdered! Who wouldn't have a few to calm himself? And anyway I don't need to make excuses. When I have a drink is my business! And I don't need anyone to tell me what time it is."

Charlie Swicegood shook his head almost imperceptibly, but it was enough for Frankie to understand that Lan Franco was lying. The oilman was already imbibing when Swicegood arrived. The sign of a true alcoholic, she thought: lying about his drinking. Soon that facade of health and vigor would collapse around a withered old man, and everyone would be amazed by his sudden decline.

"I'm putting up a reward in the morning," Lan Franco said angrily. "Twenty-five thousand. And I don't care if they drag the bastard back here in three pieces." He paused and then added quietly, "Claudine was the best. Sweet, thoughtful, generous. Who'd do this? Why didn't he just steal the valuables and leave? If Curtis were still alive it would've been different. He'd've had the bastard for the dogs' dinner."

Gregory Taylor and Congressman Jake Taylor walked into the police station together. They obviously had been talking outside, and they continued their quiet conversation as they came through the door. Neither seemed particularly upset, and Frankie thought that they might well be discussing the state of the economy or Jake's chances for election to the Senate rather than the bloody murder of their mother. They broke off the conversation and turned to wait for the heavy-set man who had entered the room shortly behind them.

"You all know Edgar Brooks, my campaign manager, don't you?" Jake Taylor said. But before anyone could respond he added, "Damn! Mother dead! Hard to believe!"

Brooks stepped protectively in front of his candidate. He was a short man with a thick bull neck, a boxer's ruined nose, and a massive belly that hung over and almost obscured a brass belt buckle in the shape of a longhorn steer. He thrust his chin forward and it appeared for a moment that he was about to take charge of the proceedings, but instead he began to shake his head slowly. "Pitiful, pitiful night," he said. "Hard to understand. Makes you realize what's really important. Puts things in perspective." He laid a surprisingly dainty hand on Jake Taylor's arm. "I didn't know your mother that well, Jake. It seems like all those times we've been out to Fairfield it was always you and me talking business or politics. I didn't get to know her. I'm sure she was a grand lady." He paused and took several deep breaths. The excitement and his weight were against him and he used his free hand to brush back the sweat that had begun to form on his broad forehead. After a few seconds he said, "Whatever you need, Jake. Anything. I'll take care of it. I'm available. Okay?"

"Okay, Edgar," Jake replied. "I appreciate it."

Frankie watched the solicitous political advisor and thought that she had never seen anyone who was quite so *attentive*. All the while he had been talking, his eyes had been darting about the room, taking in everything and everyone. She had met him before, at various political functions, but had never really observed him closely until now. He was a physically repulsive man, about five feet eight, 230 pounds at least, and he definitely had a touch of the sleaze-ball about him. But he also had power, presence. While he was speaking, no one in the room had seemed inclined to interrupt him. She knew that he was a relative newcomer to East Texas, imported from Baton Rouge within the year by Congressman Taylor to serve first as his factotum, and then, after the Senate announcement, as his campaign manager. She wondered why Taylor had not chosen a nationally known figure to head up his drive for the Senate, instead of a second-rate lobbyist from Louisiana. But no sense trying to understand it. The logic of Southern politicians was amorphous. Look at the men who took Jimmy Carter to national prominence.

James Lan Franco walked toward Jake and Gregory. "Sorry, kids," he said. "Tough way to lose your mother. Your dad and I always tried to look after her, to protect her. But it seems when she needed us most, neither of us was around. . . . But at least she and Curtis are together now. That's something."

Gregory Taylor frowned. "Save the religious crap for the funeral, Uncle Jim. Anyway, it doesn't suit you. Your God's in your hip pocket. Mom was the religious one. God knows *she* was religious."

"Come on, Greg," said Jake Taylor, "take it easy. Now's not the time."

"Always the politician, eh, Jake?" Greg said with a disdainful chuckle. He shrugged. "Winnie?"

"Haven't found her yet," said Blackie. "Looks like we'll have to wait until later to tell her."

Greg smiled. "Good old Winnie. At least she's always known exactly what she wants."

Edgar Brooks shrugged disgustedly and said, "What is all this? Let's knock it off, shall we, and get to the point! Have you forgotten, Greg, that your mother's dead?"

"I haven't forgotten anything," Greg shot back. "And butt out, okay? Go the hell back to Longview! This is family. What've you got to do with it?"

The campaign manager grew red in the face and looked for a moment as if he was going to cuff the disrespectful young man out the door; but after narrowing his eyes and smiling coldly, he turned to Blackie Boone. "Chief, could you fill us in on the details of Claudine's murder? We seem to be straying here. What have you got so far?"

Blackie took about five minutes to bring them up to date. Then he added, "Judge Moreno and Dr. Presley are finishing up at Fairfield. They're probably on their way back with the body by now."

Lan Franco said in a controlled voice that barely concealed his rage, "I'm offering a twenty-five thousand dollar reward. Whoever did this is probably in Dallas by now, but I want him and I'll get him."

Jake Taylor ignored his uncle and said to Blackie, "You'll have to know what was taken—maybe we can make up a list for you tomorrow. The safe was wide open, you say? I'm not sure what she kept in there anymore. There was a robbery two years ago, you remember. They got into the safe that time, too. I think Mother took most of her things out of the house after that. At least I advised her to. The jewelry's at the bank. Was anything left in the safe?"

"Insurance papers," Blackie replied, "car titles, property deeds, oil leases, stock certificates . . . no money, no jewelry.

If there *was* anything negotiable in there, he got it. Well, wait a minute. He missed some bearer bonds, but I don't think this guy was smart enough to know how to handle that kind of thing, so he just left them. He went through the cupboard and drawers like a tornado—stuff all over the floor. The silver's still there. I guess that tells us he was traveling light—fast. He didn't want anything that would slow him down. As I see it, he breaks into the house—we're not sure how or where—quietly pulls a few drawers, pokes around downstairs for a while, doesn't find much, and goes upstairs. He slips into Claudine's bedroom, where he pulls a few more drawers, and then looks into the closet, where he sees the safe. That sets him off. He smells big money. He drags Claudine out of bed and forces the combination out of her. For what it's worth it looks like she put up quite a fight—maybe she tried to run—because we found her body in the upstairs hallway. Anyway, he writes the combination down on a small slip of paper. . . . Then he kills her, opens the safe and tosses the slip of paper on top. He's not satisfied with what he finds, so he rampages through the rest of the house, throwing open cupboards and yanking drawers—wildly now, because he knows he's committed murder and wants something big to show for it."

"How do we know he didn't tear up the house first?" Frankie asked.

"Well, we don't know, really. But from the looks of the place he wasn't too quiet about it—some of the drawers are ten, fifteen feet from the bureaus, like he tossed them. Not very logical that he quietly pulls a drawer—afraid to wake up Claudine—and then gently carries it across the room and places it upside down. No, a few drawers and cupboards first, then up to the bedroom, torture, murder, the safe, and then the rampage."

Charlie Swicegood said, "That's the way I see it, too, Chief. I was the first one out there. The back door was standing wide open. From the phone call and everything, I couldn't have missed the son of a bitch by more than a couple of minutes. Crafty bastard, though. There's only one road out of Fairfield—clear up to the highway. He couldn't have made it that far before I came down there. He must've pulled off the farm road—no lights—and waited for me to fly past. Then he was out to the highway and gone. When I got inside I knew I was going to find something bad. The dogs was madder'n hell like they knew what had happened." He turned to Jake and Greg and placed a giant, meaty hand on Greg's shoulder. "I'll tell you one thing, if that guy'd still been in the house, he'd be down at the hospital now, and to hell with his Miranda rights. I'd've shoved that Miranda card down his throat and pulled it out his ass. Your mother was special around here. A good churchgoin' lady. Helped a lot of folks."

"She was churchgoin' all right, Charlie," Greg said. "Always was. But in the last couple of years she thought of nothing else. Mass every morning. Sixty-five years old and all the way into town every morning. You couldn't talk to her but she was fiddling with those damn beads."

"It was her heart," said Jake Taylor. "You get a bad heart like Mother and see how fast you start getting religious."

"Not me," said Greg. "I don't buy any of that voodoo mumbo jumbo. And besides, what the hell kind of Catholic church have we got in this town? Whoever heard of a Catholic church with healing services—tongues, that sort of thing? What do they call it—charismatic? Sounds like something out of Tulsa, Oklahoma, or someplace. Catholics are supposed to light candles, not jump up and down like a bunch of neurotics."

"Mother liked it, needed it," Jake said.

Greg nodded. "That she did. That she did."

4

As Father Robert Stickney prepared for Monday morning Mass, he experienced a contradiction of feelings. He was pleased to see the large number of worshippers waiting in the chapel. There were at least forty present (ten to twelve of whom were men—more than usual, and a step in the right direction); and he knew that many of the largest parishes in Texas could not draw anywhere near forty at 7:00 A.M. on a Monday morning. But he also felt an overwhelming sadness. He had just learned of Claudine Taylor's murder, and Mass, on Monday morning or any other day, would never be the same again. Claudine was a faithful member of the flock, and indeed one of his most beloved sheep—one of those original ten from the Longview parish who had responded instantly to his suggestion that Catholics had every bit as much right as Pentecostals or anyone else to participate in God's charisma.

What a dreadful death she must have endured. Her last night on earth must have been one of unrelieved horror.

He completed his vesting and stepped out to begin his march to the altar. The entrance hymn, which had been chosen to reflect an ecstatic theme, did nothing to lift his spirits; nor did the dialogue of the joyful greeting. But as he led the worshippers into the abrupt change from the penitential rite, he felt at last that the true theme of the Mass had been reached: sorrow. Sorrow for sins, sorrow for faults, sorrow for Claudine Taylor. Lord have mercy, Christ have mercy, Lord have mercy.

After the gospel and response, he straightened his vestments and, as was his habit, moved forward several paces to confront his flock more directly. He was about to embark upon his usual ten-minute homily when the loss of Claudine Taylor suddenly became unbearably real to him and deeply personal. He felt his eyes swelling, his face burning, and his emotions demanding release. He threw back his head and ejaculated a long, steady stream of what an outsider would have heard as gibberish, but what he was convinced was a heavenly language.

A middle-aged woman rose immediately (almost before he had finished) and shouted, "God is holy—experience His presence. Begin again . . . openness."

Father Stickney lowered his head, sweat dripping in great drops down his brow and onto his neck. But almost as quickly as the original release had come, he now regained control and resumed the Mass.

After the blessing and the dismissal, he visited briefly outside with several lingering church members, and then reentered the chapel. He looked around to make certain that no stragglers were still inside, and then fell to his knees at the altar, alternately praying and weeping and speaking in tongues.

Thirty minutes later he rose (once again under perfect control), smoothed his garments, and walked toward the side door of the chapel, which led to a small suite of offices.

The first sight that greeted him as he entered his study was the barrel of a shotgun.

"Hello, Pastor," the man holding the weapon said calmly.

Father Stickney nodded. His eyes were steady.

"I think you have something I want."

"And what might that be?"

"What you were given at Fairfield."

". . . So you're the one who killed Claudine."

"Yes." He leveled the shotgun. "And I think you know why I'm here now."

Stickney said nothing.

"You'll be more cooperative before we're through . . . I promise you that."

"If I am, will you let me live?"

"You're a dead man, Pastor."

"Then why should I tell you anything?"

The man smiled coldly and said, "Because if you don't you'll die slowly—a piece at a time. Cooperate, and you go to your God quickly. No pain. The twinkling of an eye, so to speak."

Father Stickney did not answer, but closed his eyes and raised his head toward the ceiling. "Father in heaven, forgive—"

The shotgun's blast shook the room.

If the man's intention was to wound the priest, he was guilty of a terrible miscalculation. He had greatly underestimated the power of his weapon at close range. The shell ripped through Stickney's shoulder, tearing away the arm and leaving a gory, tremulous stump; but the shot also spread to the neck, gouging out a four-inch section of jugular. Father Stickney died before he hit the floor.

The man examined the body and then cursed aloud his bad judgment. Next he began opening drawers and filing cabinets, emptying the contents on the floor, and reaching in back of each drawer and cabinet to make certain that nothing was taped behind or underneath.

Winnie Taylor stood outside the entrance to the Ramada Inn Coffee Shop talking to Officer Charlie Swicegood. What she had just been told had caused her to lower her head and to slump against the doorway.

"Mother murdered," she cried softly. "No, it can't be."

"Yes, it's true," he said. "I'm very sorry, Miss Taylor."

"When . . . who?"

"Last night. Looks like around eleven o'clock. We don't know who, but we've got a pretty good idea it was a burglar. Caught her alone out there. You kids all gone and the servants on vacation. We tried to find you, to tell you, but —"

"I was out at the lake."

"Where?"

"Does that matter?"

"Yes, it does. But you don't have to go into it now if you don't want to."

"Jake, Greg?"

"Greg's at his place. Jake took Edgar Brooks back to Long-view—but he's probably out at Fairfield by now."

"Uncle Jim?"

"Home. He's going out to Fairfield later. He's talking about putting up a reward. Your mother's over at Marsh's Funeral Home. But I wouldn't recommend going over there yet. They'll need some time to . . . well, frankly, Miss Taylor, they'll need some time to fix her up. I'm afraid she wasn't a pretty sight."

"Did Mother suffer?"

"Yes, I'm afraid so."

She lowered her head again.

"Will you be all right?"

She nodded. "I'll go over to Greg's for now."

"Let us know if you need anything," he said gently. He encircled both of her folded arms with one huge hand. "I'm awfully sorry to have to tell you this way—and so late. I hate to have you just standing here. Can I drive you over to Greg's place?"

"No, I have my car."

"Then I'd better go on. I've got to round up Mayor Hogan. Couldn't find him last night, either."

Winnie Taylor's expression remained heavy, but she managed the hint of a smile.

5

FRANCESCA Mills woke early Monday afternoon with the feeling that she still had a great deal left to do. It was not a feeling that was common to her on a Monday after the paper had been put to bed. Usually she felt a sense of relief and accomplishment, mixed with the need to drift aimlessly, at least until Tuesday morning. But this afternoon was different. She had better get up and get rolling; the murder of Claudine Taylor (the mother of a United States congressman who was in the middle of a heated Senate race) was not a story that could be neglected. If she was not careful reporters from . . . she sat up abruptly in bed. Dammit! What the hell was the matter with her? This *was* a national news story. Kilkenny was probably swarming with wire service reporters. She might already be too late. How could she be thinking of next Monday's edition of the *Kilkenny Weekly Times?* If she dug in fast enough, she might be able to cover the story for one of the wire services, or for a New York or Washington paper. She'd better get on the horn, call Mike Winchester, her old boss at *The New York Times.* She could wrap it all up later, at a leisurely pace, for the Kilkenny yokels. A week was an eternity for a newspaper. The big boys must be screaming for copy right now.

She swung her legs out from the bed and stretched a long arm toward the nightstand. But before she could reach the telephone, she jerked her arm back like a taut piece of rubber. She screamed and then screamed again. The pain shot along her arm and raced across her shoulder and down her back, where it attacked the base of her spine. She fell sobbing to her knees. While on her knees she doubled over and screamed again, her hands clutching her abdomen.

Recovered now, she sat in the common waiting room of the Tyler Diagnostic Clinic. The sign on the nearest door said: DR. YOGI ISHIKAWA—NEPHROLOGY. She had been seated for only a few moments when a large woman with a warm smile opened the door and said, "Frankie, come on in. Dr. Ishikawa will see you immediately."

"Thanks, Norma. It hasn't been a good day." She rose slowly and followed the nurse through the door, stopping briefly to brace herself on the inside wall of the inner waiting room.

"Are you all right?" Norma said, hurrying over to support her. "You said on the phone you were doing better."

"Yes, I'm fine now. Just a little shaky. I'm sorry to be such a baby." She grimaced as she spoke, and it was apparent that the pain had not yet disappeared completely.

"Hello, Mrs. Mills." A stern-faced young doctor had exited one of the treatment rooms and was already examining her carefully with his eyes.

"Good afternoon, Dr. Ishikawa," she replied somewhat stiffly. The serious-minded internist did not invite informality and that suited her just fine. "A bad time, I'm afraid. Almost as bad as two months ago, but not quite. If it ever gets that bad again, I think I'd just as soon die."

Ishikawa did not respond, as she knew he wouldn't. He always left any remarks that even hinted at self-pity or self-absorption unanswered, unacknowledged, as if they were completely outside his area of responsibility. She thought she knew why, though she had never discussed it with him (one didn't discuss *anything* extraneous with Dr. Ishikawa). She was certain it was because he had spent his residency and the first fifteen years of his career at M.D. Anderson Hospital in Houston, specializing in pediatric urinary cancer.

After dealing with those brave little souls for so many years, he must have had no patience left for whining adults who couldn't face the realities of a cruel and unjust world. She breathed heavily and resolved to make no other indulgent comments.

Dr. Ishikawa asked brusquely, "Are you checking your flow regularly?"

Frankie nodded thoughtfully. "I believe so, Doctor."

"Believing is not good enough! Bacteria thrive in urine. You *must* check your flow, empty frequently, keep your appliances clean! You can't allow your mind to forget!"

"Sometimes I get busy. Running a newspaper, even a small-town weekly, isn't as easy as you might think."

"Then sell the newspaper!"

Frankie frowned and said, "I was told in New York that I could lead a normal life."

"As indeed you can, Mrs. Mills," said Ishikawa. He paused for a moment, as if carefully considering his next words, and then added, "But you must understand that though your life can still be *normal,* it is also *new.* You've been given a new lease on life. Fifty years ago you'd have been dead. But your new life requires new commitments. And one of those commitments must be to properly care for your kidneys. *Anything,* Mrs. Mills, that distracts you from that commitment is a danger to your new life. If your newspaper is a distraction, then I repeat, sell it!"

"I don't think that will be necessary," she answered defensively.

Ishikawa went on, "Infection is your greatest enemy." He moved closer and in a rare gesture of warmth, touched her arm. "Have you had fever?"

"Yes, off and on for about three days."

"What about the color, the smell of your urine?"

"Dark, I'm afraid. Looks like it did before, like strong tea. It doesn't seem to have any unusual smell."

"We're going to have to have a urinalysis and a blood test, and I'm going to want another IVP."

"How long will all of this take?" Frankie asked. "I've got an important story breaking back in Kilkenny." She watched as the doctor's mouth tightened and then added quickly, "Congressman Taylor's mother was murdered last night—maybe you've heard? I—"

"I've heard," said Ishikawa coldly. He removed his hand from her arm. "But may I remind you, Mrs. Mills, that the congressman's mother is quite dead—often a permanent condition. You, on the other hand, are still alive; and it is my intention to keep you so."

"Dr. Ishikawa, I assure you that I—"

"And something else, Mrs. Mills. I'm not entirely satisfied with your file. Your progress does not please me. It's been over a year and a half now since your cystectomy. I realize that you've been assured that there is every reason to believe that the cancer was not pervasive. And that may very well be true. But remember *this*. When a malignancy is extensive enough to require removal of the entire bladder, extreme care has to be taken at every post-operative stage to insure the truth of any assessment."

Frankie had gone white. "What do you mean?" she asked quietly.

The internist softened his tone. "I don't wish to frighten you—except insofar as to get you to take better care of yourself—but there are several other tests that I'd like to make: the ovaries, the fallopian tubes, the uterus—the kidneys themselves; there may be more than recurring infection involved here. The pain is very persistent and, if I may say, very suspicious. How is your weight, by the way? Of course I'll have Norma check, but you *do* look a little gaunt."

"I've lost seven more pounds this month."

Ishikawa nodded. "Any malignancy in the kidneys is very difficult to diagnose, but I believe it's time to get started—at least to eliminate that possibility."

Frankie shrugged. "You don't pull any punches, do you?"

"You're the kind of woman who needs them full-strength. . . . I want the pyelogram, arteriography, muscle and bowel tissue samples—everything. I want to know all there is to know about you. We should be through by the end of the week."

So much for the Claudine Taylor murder story, Frankie thought. "What happens," she said, "if a tumor *is* found in one of my kidneys?"

"That depends—possibly surgery."

"Removal?"

"Again that depends. With your history a nephrectomy is a very real possibility."

"What if both kidneys are involved?"

"You must have at least one kidney to live. But we're getting ahead of ourselves. We don't know anything yet."

"They did all of these tests in New York, you know," Frankie said.

Ishikawa shook his head. "I'm afraid not. At least not all that I intend to do. And even if they had, I'd still want them done again. The body changes, Mrs. Mills."

Frankie said cynically, "A forty-year-old kid in Tyler, Texas, is going to improve on the work of one of the most respected specialists in the most sophisticated city in the world."

Dr. Ishikawa did not answer, but handed Frankie's chart to his nurse. He walked quietly from the room.

"Goddamn, he's a cold bastard!" Frankie said.

"You *do* know, don't you," said Norma, "that every major hospital in the world would like to get Dr. Ishikawa—including the Memorial Sloan-Kettering Cancer Center in New York?"

"I know," said Frankie, smiling weakly. "They're the ones who gave me his name. I was just being a stupid son of a bitch. An old habit of mine."

Norma came closer and said warmly, "Let's have a look at that stoma, and then get you started on those tests. Also, before you leave, I'm sure the doctor will give you something stronger for the pain."

It was past five when Frankie arrived back in Kilkenny. She went straight to City Hall, and was startled by the enormous crowd milling about outside. As she drove closer she recognized reporters from *The Houston Post, The Dallas Morning News,* and the *Austin American Statesman;* and she was certain that the rest were in the business, too. No one *waited* quite like a reporter—the bored slouch, the surly expression, the feline readiness. The wire services, the national newsmagazines, and the Eastern newspapers appeared to be amply represented. There was no other explanation for the horde of well-dressed young people lined up along the sidewalk and spilling over onto the grass. She scanned their smooth, tanned faces and found none that she knew. She chuckled to herself. She guessed that her former friends in New York and Washington were getting too long in the tooth to travel about the country on assignment. It was becoming a business of attractive, well-connected journalism school graduates who had their eyes fixed firmly on television news and who were using print journalism merely as a means to fatten their résumés. She wondered how many of them could actually write. She'd wager that there was a large number of harried copy editors at *Time* and *Newsweek* and *The Washington Post* who were rending their clothes in frustration over the incoherent stories submitted by these handsome youngsters.

Well, the murder story belonged to them now, at least the hot releases and fast-breaking news. No sense calling Mike Winchester in New York. With all of the tests that the arrogant little bastard, Ishikawa, had ordered, she'd be lucky to be able to get her own story prepared for next Monday's edition of the *Kilkenny Weekly Times.*

She parked her car a full block from City Hall, the only spot she could find, and began to walk, somewhat unsteadily, through the alley toward the front of the building. She knew that the extra-strong mixture of Tylenol and codeine that Dr. Ishikawa had given her was making her look like the town drunk, but there was nothing she could do about it. The air and the short walk should be enough to bring her system back to normal.

She joined the waiting crowd, and said to an acquaintance

from *The Houston Post*, "Looks more like the White House lawn than the Kilkenny, Texas City Hall."

Before the Houston reporter could answer, Chief Blackie Boone vigorously pushed open the glass front door and called out, "Frankie, where the hell have you been? I saw you walking down the alley. I've been over to your paper several times—Gabe didn't know *where* you were. Come on in!" He none too gently brushed aside several of the grumbling reporters and ushered her inside.

"The priest, too," Blackie said when they'd reached his office. "Unbelievable."

Frankie looked puzzled. "Priest?"

"You mean you don't know?"

"Know what? What're you talking about?"

"Father Robert Stickney was murdered this morning—blasted with a shotgun. Right after Monday morning Mass!"

"Stickney . . . you mean the—"

"Yeah, right. Claudine Taylor's priest. The crazy one. The one the kids call 'Fire-eyes.'"

Frankie motioned outside. "All those reporters—"

"Claudine Taylor, mostly. Her murder is all over the national news. They've been running back and forth between here and Fairfield all day. But they've picked up on the priest's killing, too. Two murders in twenty-four hours in a town the size of Kilkenny makes them stop and wonder."

"Do you think the two murders are related?"

"Don't have any idea. We kind of thought that Claudine's killer took off right away. But this could be a whole new ball game now."

"Why?"

"Well, there were some similarities—not to mention the coincidence of two quick murders. For one thing, both killings were extremely violent. Sure, the methods were different, but violence is violence, and neither one was done with a light touch. This guy seems to like what he does. For another, Father Stickney's office looks just like Claudine's place. Everything was ransacked like the guy was looking for something."

"Valuables?"

"Could be. But that doesn't quite sit right in my little country brain. When things start happening in pairs, I begin to get fidgety. There's a whole bunch of things worth looking into here."

For the first time since she'd met Blackie Boone, Frankie looked carefully at his face as he spoke. What she saw surprised her. Even though his fleshy cheeks and broad grin had squeezed his eyes into thin slits, she could still see—unmistakably—the bright gleam of intelligence.

"Pairs and threesomes," she said.

Blackie didn't hesitate. "You mean Karen Erikson's suicide. I thought of that. *Three* violent deaths are even more troublesome. Makes me wonder what the hell's going on. I'll tell you one thing, though."

"What's that?"

"I mean to find out."

6

MAYOR Beaker Hogan often used his office at City Hall for double duty. Since the Kilkenny mayor's job was a part-time responsibility and the pay negligible, and since by serving he was neglecting his law firm, he felt justified in conducting much of his legal business from the mayor's office.

On his glass-topped desk lay Claudine Taylor's will, which had been in effect for over ten years and which distributed all of her earthly goods equally among her three children. Beside it lay a handwritten letter that he had just reread for the third time—not because he wasn't familiar with its contents (it had dominated his thoughts for over a week now), but because he was trying intently to visualize Claudine Taylor as she wrote it. He concentrated deeply and pictured her at her writing table: a piece of stationery headed C. T.—Fairfield; an inkwell; an old-fashioned pen; the letter; the envelope and stamp. He repeated the process several times, each time straining to focus the images more clearly in his mind.

He picked up the letter and walked to the window, where he stood staring at the well-kept lawn below. He nodded several times, slowly, contemplatively—as if confirming to himself a conclusion he had already reached. There can't be a carbon, he thought. It would be completely illogical. No one—not even a meticulous old lady like Claudine Taylor—would use a piece of carbon paper for a handwritten note.

This had to be the only copy of the letter, and he had to be
the only one who had seen it.

He read it through once again:

C. T.—Fairfield

Dear Beaker,

*I want to make some changes in my will. This
will give you some time to do the preliminary
work.*

*My intention is to leave the bulk of my estate
to St. Andrew's Chapel—naming Father Robert
Stickney as sole executor.*

*I'd like some words included to the effect that
this does not indicate any lack of love for my
three children. As you know, Jake was well
provided for in his father's will. Please make
reference to this. You know how sensitive
political constituencies can be. They'd read
disinheritance as disapproval, and I want it
made clear that I approve of Jake entirely.*

*Greg and Winnie, however, are another matter
altogether. I want them specifically left out! I've
given this a great deal of thought, and I'm doing
this for their own good.*

*Greg has always led a rootless, pointless life,
and now he seems to be wrapped up in these
anti-nuclear, anti-this and anti-that things—
and I simply do not want my money to go
toward the support of ideas that I don't agree
with.*

*And as for Winnie, I want her to have to get
out and work—period! She reminds me of an
animal, living day to day—as if life had no
greater meaning than eating, sleeping, and
rutting!*

*Beaker, there are other reasons for my decision
to leave my money to the church, reasons that
you will discover in due time.*

*But for now, please begin to revise my will
according to these instructions. We'll work out
the details and the signing and witnessing, etc.
later.*

Affectionately,
Claudine Taylor

He made a quick decision. He returned to the desk,
reached for the cigarette lighter, and set fire to the corner of
the letter. He held it as long as he could, and when it was
half gone, he dropped the remainder in the ashtray, and
watched the flames consume the rest.

So much for the charismatic Catholics, he thought. Well,
it was too late for Father Stickney anyway. Whoever took his
place would just have to rely on the twenty or thirty other
melancholic oddballs who would surely leave their fortunes
to St. Andrew's parish. Shouldn't be too difficult to manage.

He'd say one thing for old Claudine Taylor. She had a way
with words. Describing her daughter, Winnie, as a rutting
animal was certainly apt. He shook his leonine head, laughed
quietly, and gazed out the window toward Lake Kilkenny.

Claudine Taylor's favorite flowers were wild azaleas, and
that fact was not lost on those who had decorated Marsh's
Funeral Home in her memory. One entire wall of the entrance hallway was awash in the pink and white blossoms.

The opposite wall was lined with wreaths and baskets of
many different floral varieties; these were devoted to the
memory of Father Robert Stickney.

County Judge Susan Moreno, Dr. Knox Presley, and Roy
Griddle, Marsh's proprietor, stood in the hallway between
the banks of flowers.

Dr. Presley looked at his watch. "Six o'clock," he said.
"The priest was killed this morning—about nine hours ago.
Claudine Taylor last night—eighteen, nineteen hours or so.
And look at this place! There's already more flowers here
than the Gregg County Arboretum!" He motioned toward
Claudine Taylor's wall. ". . . Or the Azalea Festival."

Judge Moreno, a dark-haired, strikingly beautiful woman in her late thirties, said, "What's the matter with that, Knox?"

Dr. Presley shrugged. "Nothing, I guess. It's just that something's missing."

Roy Griddle said, "I think I know what you mean. I've got *three* bodies here, not just two. Right?"

"Right," said Dr. Presley. "Where in the hell are Karen Erikson's flowers? You realize that there's not one goddamned maypop in this place to remind anyone that she lived or died!" He spun full circle to emphasize his words. He was obviously tired and irritated. He removed his wire-rimmed glasses, rubbed his eyes, and added, "My mother and dad used to know her. We've still got pictures in the attic: picnics, things like that. Mom, Dad, me—I was just a baby—and Karen and her husband, Samuel. Karen was as pretty as a movie star, corn-colored hair, perfect figure, wide grin—as if she didn't have a care in the world. He sighed dejectedly. "*Now* go in there and look at her!" He pointed toward the room that contained the corpses. "A broken-down old derelict. Mom and Dad never did know why she left town after Samuel died. She just up and left—a few months later. Didn't tell anybody anything. My folks talked about it for years. I guess I could've picked up some flowers for her—should have. In fact, by God, I think I will!"

Roy Griddle yawned, stretched his tall, slim, undertaker's frame, and said to Susan Moreno, "What next, Judge? Are we keeping the bodies?"

"No," she replied, "I'm sending them all to the Dallas M.E.'s office."

"I can do these autopsies," Dr. Presley said. "I've done hundreds."

"Car crashes and hunting accidents," said Judge Moreno. "This is different, Knox. You know that. You're not even a pathologist. We're going to do this right."

"Karen Erikson, too?"

"Her, too. After all, we have nothing but her note to assure us her death was really suicide. That might have been enough before, but it's not any longer."

In Longview, Edgar Brooks, Jake Taylor's campaign manager, sat naked and dispirited in his study. He felt old, worn. He wondered with amusement how he could expect to feel at sixty (a presumptuous forecast) if he felt this way at forty-nine. He knew he was desperately out of shape: great rolls of fat bulged across his middle, his legs were a smear of burst veins; and even though he had been resting for some minutes, his breath came in short gasps.

He mopped his brow with the end of one of the overstuffed chair's arm covers, and reached for a cigarette. Why did he always hitch his wagon to one man? Why couldn't he branch out a little—run two or three political candidates, like a fight manager with several different boxers. If a contender goes down and *stays* down, the fight manager doesn't stay down with him, he simply moves on to the next man. It should be that way in Washington. Politicians were just false fronts anyway, dummies to mouth other men's ideas and policies. The string pullers shouldn't collapse when the marionettes collapse.

But reality was reality. Jake Taylor was his meal ticket, his big chance. It was now or never: Jake Taylor the Senator (with Edgar Brooks whispering in his ear the whole way), or Jake Taylor the loser (with Edgar Brooks back scrounging second- and third-rate lobbying assignments in Austin and Baton Rouge).

The phone beside his right hand rang, and he answered it immediately.

"Mr. Edgar Brooks, please."

"Brooks speaking."

"Mr. Brooks, this is the office of the President of the United States. The President would like to talk to you for a few moments. Will you please hold?"

He jerked instantly upright, and brought his bare legs together as if he'd been discovered sprawled naked in the

Oval Office. "Of course, I'll hold," he said. It was an unnecessary response, since the President's secretary had assumed just that and was already off the line.

"Edgar," the President said, "how are you? How're things in Texas?"

"Yes, hello, Mr. President. Nice to talk to you again. . . . About as well as can be expected, I suppose."

"Terrible thing about Jake's mother. I called him earlier."

"Yes, yes, you did. I know you did, Mr. President. He called me from his mother's place."

"Edgar . . . do you see any possible damage to the party in this tragic murder? We don't want to lose that Senate seat. We need it to insure our majority and our programs for the next session."

"I understand, Mr. President. No. No, I don't see any possible damage to the party here. Everything is proceeding in an orderly manner. This may even (and please excuse my callousness—but politics is politics) enhance Jake's chances for election in November. The sympathy vote, you know."

After a long pause the President said, "Thank you, Edgar. Keep me informed, will you? And by the way, Edgar, be sure to let me know the next time you're in Washington. I'd like to have you drop by. There's three or four of my people I'd like you to meet."

"Yes, sir," Edgar replied eagerly. "The next time, sir!"

He replaced the receiver and sat very still. His heart had begun to pound wildly. He could actually feel the blood racing to his arms, and his hands and his legs and his toes and his face. He threw his head back on the chair and stared at the ceiling. Satisfaction . . . in the deepest sense of the word. The President of the United States calling Edgar Brooks. And that's as it should be—and would be. It had taken a long time, but at last he was beginning to move in the circles where his intelligence and awareness would be appreciated and recognized. The President of the United States. Goddamn! Drop by the White House next time you're in Washington, would you, Edgar? Yes, Mr. President, I believe I will!

He leapt energetically to his feet. He felt light-headed, vibrant. He danced his huge, naked body across the room to the drink table. He poured himself a Jack Daniels and water, and toasted aloud, "The only way to live! No more state-capital lobbying for Edgar Brooks." But as he gulped down his drink, he remembered the problems he still faced, and his elation vanished.

The front door to Lan Franco Villa stood nine feet ten inches tall and was fashioned of pure cypress. The panels were hand-carved and contained a myriad of figures, all depicting ships and other aspects of the seafaring life. Not that James Lan Franco had any particular interest in the sea. The carvings were the idea of his cabinetmaker, a former ship's carpenter, whom Lan Franco had brought in to attend to the finishing touches on his mansion. His only instructions to the craftsman had been to "make it big, and make it gaudy! I want people to know who the hell's door they're at!"

To that extent at least, the cabinetmaker had succeeded. The door was certainly gaudy. And James's wife, Beta, hated it. She hated the way it screamed to everyone about to enter that the house's occupants had no taste at all. For over twenty years she had tried vainly to get her husband to exchange it for a quiet, tasteful door, one that would speak of the simple and subdued furnishings that she had managed to accumulate over the years. But although James had allowed her to have her way within the house, he remained stubborn on the matter of the door, and no amount of wheedling would change his mind. "I'm surprised you don't put a giant rack of deer horns over the damned thing!" she had said, exasperated. "Not a bad idea," he replied. "I'll give it some thought." She took this as her cue not to nag him any further, and tried to remain content with what she had accomplished inside.

But as the two returned from Fairfield and stood on their porch, it was obvious that the issue had not been resolved. James watched his wife's eyes roam disgustedly over the intricate carvings, and he chuckled quietly. "Claudine and Curtis always wanted a door like this," he said.

"Curtis maybe, never Claudine. She had too much taste. You and Curtis were two of a kind."

He turned his key in the lock. "I'll admit to that. One of the best brothers-in-law in the world and one of the best friends I've ever had. When he died a lot of me went with him. A lot of me went with Claudine, too," he added sadly. "Guess for a while there won't be much of me left."

She touched his arm. "I'm so sorry about Claudine, Jim. A horrible way to die. Your only sister . . . Maybe if we'd had children it wouldn't have been so bad. Your love would've been more spread out, so to speak."

"Maybe." He nodded. He strode purposefully toward a large cabinet just inside the study.

Beta frowned and said, "Jim, you haven't stopped drinking all day. Are you going to drink all night, too?"

"I will if I goddamned want to!" he said, slamming the unfilled glass down on the bar. He poured it defiantly full of bourbon and went on, "My sister murdered, and you get on my ass over a few goddamned drinks!"

"I'm not on your ass, and you started this constant drinking *before* she was killed. You haven't been sober since Saturday night—when that horrible Erikson creature came to see you. What did she *do* to upset you so much? I read about her in the paper. You didn't tell me she used to live in Kilkenny. I don't remember her."

He replied softly, "Before I brought you down here, Beta, Claudine, Curtis, and I used to pal around with her and her husband Samuel. After he died she left."

"You never mentioned her."

"I never thought about it."

"What did she want with you Saturday night? You said you'd tell me, but you were drinking all night Saturday and all day Sunday, and then—Claudine! Why'd Karen Erikson come here?"

He drained his bourbon glass and sat down heavily in a black leather chair.

"She was just touching all the bases, I guess," he said, ". . . before she took that acid. She'd seen Claudine earlier Saturday and old Mrs. Embry from the school." He stumbled about for additional words and then mumbled under his breath, "pilgrimage."

7

THE crowd of reporters had deserted City Hall for
Fairfield, and at 11:00 P.M. showed no signs of dis-
persing. There were three television trucks parked
in the circular gravel driveway. Bright lights illuminated
the grounds, and impatient commentators and reporters
slouched sullenly, waiting for someone concerned with the
case to appear at the floodlit entranceway.

The front door stood slightly open and the sights and
sounds from the lawn were streaming into the house.

Behind the door in the marble-floored hallway, Francesca
Mills listened as Chief of Police Blackie Boone expressed his
thanks to Jake, Greg, and Winnie Taylor for their coopera-
tion during the past several hours. He also apologized for
the time, explaining that it was the press of two murder
investigations that had necessitated such a late arrival.

The house was very cold—the air conditioning had been
blowing for the entire time they had been inside—and Frankie was grateful for the surge of warm air she could feel
through the small opening in the door.

"I'm not going back outside," said Jake Taylor, motioning
toward the clamor on the lawn. "I can't face another reporter tonight. I've answered every possible question. Why
don't they just pack up and go home? We'll be here tomorrow."

"You want me to shoo them off, Jake?" Officer Charlie

Swicegood asked. "They're on your property. They'll have to back up to the road at least."

Jake said thoughtfully, "No, Charlie, we can't do that. I'm a United States congressman; my life's a public affair, I'm afraid. And, to be honest with you, I just can't afford to antagonize the press. I've got a five-month Senate campaign ahead of me."

Greg Taylor shrugged disdainfully.

"They won't bother me," said Winnie Taylor. "My old room's in the rear of the house. I can't hear a thing back there. I'm going to bed." She turned abruptly and walked into the living room.

Frankie watched her leave and felt a pang of jealousy at the young woman's good looks and healthy vitality.

When Winnie had disappeared, Frankie turned her attention to the others. All looked tired, and all seemed ready to bring the evening to a close. She was glad she couldn't see her own face. She sensed that she looked like hell. She was sure that dark bags were hanging under her eyes, and that deep lines were showing on her brow and around her mouth.

She looked up and saw that Blackie Boone was staring at her. He reached for her arm and said quietly, "Frankie, are you all right?"

She recoiled sharply, irritated by the intimate contact and the unsought solicitude, and said, "I'm *fine*, dammit! Tired, but fine!"

The others missed the interplay, and Jake Taylor said, "This place will have to be sold. Mother should've moved to town long ago. She'd still be alive if she had."

Blackie, whose eyes were still fixed on Frankie, replied, "Maybe, Jake. Maybe not."

"What the devil does that mean?" said Greg Taylor, puzzled. "That bastard got her because she was all alone out here!"

"We'll talk more about it tomorrow," said Blackie.

Jake and Greg Taylor both appeared to have questions,

but Blackie precluded them by opening the front door wider, thus allowing the outside noise to overpower the conversation.

Jake and Greg withdrew a few paces, and Blackie said, "Good night, see you tomorrow. We'll take care of the reporters." He pushed Frankie and Charlie outside, and then followed them, pulling the door shut behind him.

Actually, at Blackie's urging it was Frankie who dealt with the press. She answered their protests concerning her presence inside the house by explaining that she was an old friend of the family. She then suggested that since there was little more to be gained by hanging around, they all go to bed and resume their tasks in the morning.

When Frankie, Blackie, and Charlie stood beside the two patrol cars, Charlie said, "You're right, Blackie. No burglar killed Claudine. It gnawed on me all day, too. Someone who knew the area. Friend or family, eh?"

"Well, he sure as hell wasn't a transient. He knew the area all right. As to whether he was friend or family—we don't know that yet."

"What're you two talking about?" asked Frankie impatiently.

"Get in," said Blackie. "I'll show you on the way back."

Charlie Swicegood said good night and got into his car. He spun his tires on the gravel driveway and roared off toward town.

When Blackie and Frankie were seated in the chief's car, Frankie shrugged and said, "Now, what's this all about? Where are you taking me?"

"I'm not taking you anywhere until you tell me what's wrong with you," he answered firmly. "You're hurting, that's obvious, and you're hurting bad."

"It's none of your business!" she snapped. "You're not my goddamned guardian!"

"No, but I'm the one who's going to take you back to town. Or maybe you'd rather walk?"

"I can get a ride with any one of those reporters, you know that."

He nodded, and then turned the key and started the engine. "Sorry to meddle," he said slowly. "I'll try to butt out." He spun his tires even more than Swicegood had, and sped out to the farm road.

Frankie softened and said, "No big deal. I've got a minor kidney infection. Hurts like hell. I didn't know it showed."

"It shows."

"Blackie, I really do appreciate your making me a part of all of this. I want to devote most or all of next Monday's paper to these deaths. The complete story. Knock their socks off in New York. But let's keep it professional. Don't be so protective. You're Kilkenny's Chief of Police and I own the *Kilkenny Weekly Times.* Common ground, but that's it. Okay?"

"Okay," he said, shrugging. "Now do you want to see why Charlie and I decided it wasn't an out-of-towner who murdered Claudine?"

"Of course I do."

"Then watch," he said, jamming the accelerator to the floor. "Watch the right side of the road."

She turned her head to the window and stared at the passing fields. After several miles with no conversation, he brought the patrol car to a screeching halt.

"What'd you see?" he asked.

"Nothing. Fields—open fields."

"See any cutoffs, any place to pull off the road to wait for another car to come up to Fairfield from the highway?"

"No—none."

"Let's go back." This time he drove very slowly, not more than ten or fifteen miles an hour. "Now, look over here to your left. What do you see now?"

"A road. All grown over. I couldn't see it before. We were going too fast. I can barely make it out now."

"Right. And if you were racing away from Fairfield after murdering Claudine Taylor, do you think you'd drive fifteen miles per hour on the odd chance that there *might* be a side road along here? Not likely. The fields are all open—no place to hide. The pine forests don't start until you're out on the highway. That little road, though, goes on down the field and into a gully. You can't see the gully from here. You'd never know it was there—unless you knew this area."

"And that's where the killer hid?"

"Right. He must've guessed that Claudine called us—or thought she might have. He pulled off into the gully to wait for Charlie to go roaring by, and then got back on the farm road and drove to the highway. . . . The time of the telephone call, Charlie coming straight down here, there's no other answer. It should've hit me right away."

Frankie said, "This is the only road out of Fairfield, right?"

"Right."

"Then what you say is doubly logical. You know, I've been out to Fairfield four times, including tonight . . . receptions, Jake's Senate race announcement. I think I'm an observant person. I keep my eyes open, look around. But I couldn't tell you anything about these roads, crossroads, forks—anything. There could be three roads coming in here for all I know. It's not the kind of thing you pay attention to. How did the killer *know* he'd have to pull off? He knows this area all right, Blackie. He knew about that little side road and he knew there was no other way in or out of here. He knew he *had* to hide."

As she spoke she lowered her eyelids and rubbed the back of her neck with her palm.

Blackie said, "I know I'm not supposed to care, but you're hurting, and I'm getting you home."

She didn't argue, and she leaned her head wearily against the back of the seat.

8

HUMILIATION. Frankie examined her feelings again to be certain. There was no question about it. The overwhelming emotion that dominated her senses was humiliation—though she recognized a subordinate feeling of helplessness as well.

Would this runaway disintegration never end?

She stood on the steps of the Tyler Diagnostic Clinic, her face in her hands, her purse slung carelessly across her back, her legs turned awkwardly in at the knees like an insecure schoolgirl's. She was oblivious to the stares she was receiving from those passing her as they entered the clinic. Tears wet her palms and she dropped her hands to her side.

For the past three hours she had been poked, probed, and tested until she felt she had no privacy or dignity left. And there were three more such days to endure before Dr. Ishikawa could give her any definitive answer concerning her condition.

She should be used to such treatment, but she supposed one never got used to medical docility. For over two years now she had been forced to relinquish control of her body to various doctors, nurses, and technicians, each of whom was genuinely interested in her welfare, but nevertheless unable to counter her sense of personal violation.

And the greatest violation of all: the cystectomy—a year and a half ago—when the ghouls reached inside and took her bladder, leaving her a plastic bag to collect the never-ending drops of urine. God, what an abomination! No wonder Todd left. It would take an extraordinary husband indeed to—

She interrupted the thought and straightened her posture abruptly. How utterly ridiculous! She was actually standing here, making a public spectacle of herself, blaming the failure of her marriage on her cancer. A marriage that had been riddled with its own cancer for fifteen years before she had any inkling of her illness. Talk about stupidity. Of course Todd left—and good riddance—the goddamned insufferable little fart. The fact that he left after her operation was nothing more than circumstance. And if the truth were known, her sickness had probably kept them together for a year or two longer than would have been the case had she been perfectly healthy. Todd prided himself on his compassion. She shuddered as she thought of his cold smiles and oversolicitous manner.

Well, at least her ex-husband would not be around to gloat at the new verdict when it came in on Friday. She hesitated. What a dreadful choice of words—gloat. Was that what she really thought of Todd's reaction to her bladder cancer? Damn right! That's exactly what he felt. Behind those shallow, sympathetic eyes had been pure delight—no doubt about it. Well, if there was more cancer, another operation, he'd never know. He was surely still at his parent's place in Maine, and would be indefinitely, writing that goddamned eternal history of New England.

She took a deep breath and began to walk, slowly at first and then more rapidly, down the long flight of cement steps toward the parking lot.

It was nearly lunchtime when she pulled up in front of the office of the *Kilkenny Weekly Times.* She smiled in spite of herself when she saw the rotund figure of Blackie Boone seated carelessly in her chair with his feet propped in the midst of the papers on top of her desk.

"Thanks, Blackie," she said as she approached, "I appreciate you using your feet as a paperweight."

"Oh hell, Frankie, I'm sorry!" He swung his legs off the desk and sat upright in the chair. "My feet right in the middle of your things. I was just sitting here thinking. Didn't realize what I was doing."

"Where's Gabe?"

"In the bathroom trying to wash off some of that ink he's got on him."

She smiled. "It won't help. The ink on Gabe goes clear to the bone. What've you been thinking about?"

"What else? The murders. Where've you been, by the way? That's two mornings in a row you've disappeared."

"That kidney infection I told you about. I had to go to Tyler. I'm fine. It's just a question of time . . . and a few antibiotics."

He nodded. "I may be in over my head with these killings," he said slowly. "I've had offers of help from everywhere—Washington, Dallas, Houston, even Los Angeles. Every agency in the country wants in on this. Maybe I should take them up on it."

"Have you got any leads?" she asked.

"Not really. Just a few random thoughts—like what we talked about last night out on the farm road. No transient would've known about that hidden gully—or that there was no other way in or out of Fairfield. And there's the physical evidence: the knife that was used on Claudine Taylor, the antiseptic that Karen Erikson drank, the mess at St. Andrew's Chapel and Fairfield . . . Father Stickney's and Claudine's wounds, the slip of paper with the combination on it. . . . There were no fingerprints anywhere that would help us. Fingerprints are generally useless anyway—too hard to identify. And even if you do pinpoint the guy, he generally belongs around the place or can explain why his prints are there. I've been a cop for twenty-five years and I've never arrested anybody on fingerprints, and I've never heard of anyone getting arrested on fingerprints. . . . And there were no good tire tracks down in that gully or around Claudine's place. Tire tracks are more useful than fingerprints, but as I say—no help here."

"What do you mean when you say their wounds are evidence?" she asked.

Blackie sat on one edge of her desk and she sat on the other. She tossed her purse in the middle of the pile of papers in a gesture that meant she hadn't really cared about his feet being there earlier.

"The autopsies aren't complete yet," he said, "but I called the Dallas M.E.'s office twice this morning. It looks like Claudine Taylor was tortured—knife wounds in both shoulders." He paused and looked thoughtful for a moment. "Father Stickney was blasted at close range—took his arm off. No one could miss that much from that close. Looks like he was being tortured, too. Ripped his neck out by mistake."

Frankie flushed. "Why torture Father Stickney?"

"Don't have a clue. The killer was looking for something though. Now if we could show that Karen Erikson was tortured and murdered we'd really have a puzzle, wouldn't we?"

"Any evidence of that?"

"No. The M.E.'s office says she has no unusual marks, no sign of a fight or a scuffle, scratches—nothing. It's going to be hard to show that she didn't take that poison willingly."

"Maybe she did."

Gabe Sullivan returned from the washroom. The front of his face was clean, but ink still covered his sideburns and his neck.

"Hello, Mrs. Mills," he said, slipping his arms into his apron.

"Hello, Gabe," said Frankie. "Can we talk to you for a minute?"

"Sure." He came closer, and since there was no one sitting in Frankie's chair, he pulled it out and made himself comfortable. He clasped both hands behind his head and waited.

Frankie looked at Blackie and said, "Gabe and Karen Erikson's husband Samuel were friends—did you know that?"

Gabe Sullivan interrupted. "Not exactly friends. They was rich. Remember, all I said was I used to do work for old Samuel."

"How old was Samuel Erikson?" Blackie asked.

"A lot older than me," Sullivan replied. "Thirty, maybe thirty-five years older than me."

"And Karen Erikson was younger than you, wasn't she?" said Frankie.

"She was sixty-two when she died," Blackie interjected, "though she looked seventy-five—dumpy, white-headed, balding. She spent a lot of time on skid rows in Chicago and St. Louis. . . . She had receipts from cheap flophouses in both cities."

"You never told me that," said Frankie. She reached for her purse and took out a black leather notebook. While the two men waited, she jotted down what she had learned. She held the notebook ready and looked up.

Sullivan answered Frankie's question. "Right, Karen was younger than me . . . Samuel was a *whole* lot older than her—maybe forty years. He must've been close to sixty when he died. Karen was around twenty-two."

"Why'd she marry him?" Blackie asked. But he answered himself. "Silly question, eh? You've already said how rich he was."

Sullivan shrugged. "Who knows about those things?"

"I was a boy in Lufkin when all this was going on," said Blackie. "Forty years ago. I'd never heard of the Eriksons until two days ago. How'd the old man die?"

"He was murdered. Robbery. It was well known that he always carried a lot of cash—for his business. Some thief killed him just outside his office."

"What kind of business was he in?" Frankie asked.

Sullivan said, "Lumber. But that's not where I worked for him. I did chores around his house. It's that abandoned ranch off the old Dallas Highway. The road's all grown over now. I think some rancher leases those acres to run cows on."

Frankie slipped down off the corner of the desk and said, "I need some tea. How about you, Gabe? Blackie?"

Both men nodded, and Blackie got up and walked toward the small side table to help. Sullivan remained seated in

Frankie's chair. It was still very much his show, and while he was the center of attention he apparently felt it was appropriate to be served.

When Frankie and Blackie had resumed their positions on the desk, Frankie took a sip of tea and then placed her cup beside her on the stack of papers. She picked up her notebook and pen.

"Gabe," she said, "why do you think Karen Erikson came back to Kilkenny to kill herself?"

The old, ink-stained printer studied the question. Finally he replied, "I can't answer that—except to say that this might have been her last real home. From what Blackie says about the last forty years, she's been kicked around quite a bit. Maybe she just got tired and wanted to die at home."

"Do you know anything about her family, Gabe?" asked Blackie.

"Her mother was a schoolteacher. They came to town together when Karen was ten or eleven. The mother taught at the elementary school for a while. She died when Karen was a teenager. That's all the family I know about. I'll tell you one thing though. Old Bridie Embry would know all about that side of it. She taught with Karen's mother. As a matter of fact, Mrs. Embry was *my* third grade teacher. She knows *everything* about this town. She's somewhere in her nineties now, but sharp as a pin. Does all her own shopping, gardening—takes care of herself completely. I see her downtown all the time. She'll talk your head off if you'll let her. She'd know all right. . . . And you might ask Dr. Knox Presley about Karen. As I remember, his parents used to be friendly with Karen and Samuel. And James Lan Franco, try him."

"Lan Franco?" Blackie asked.

Sullivan stood and pushed Frankie's chair back under the desk. "Yeah. I guess Lan Franco's the only one of that old crowd who's still alive—except Bridie Embry—but she wasn't really a part of it. Like I told you, I used to do chores around Karen and Samuel's place and I'd see them all together: Samuel, Karen, James Lan Franco, Claudine and Curtis Taylor, and the Presleys. Seems like they were always together there for awhile."

"What about Beta Lan Franco?" Frankie asked.

"I don't know about her," said Sullivan. "I don't remember her being around. But again it's all so long ago. I *do* remember this though: Claudine Taylor was Karen Erikson's hairdresser. Claudine worked at the beauty shop. Of course all this was before Curtis and James got rich in the oilfield."

They talked for a few more minutes, but it was becoming obvious that Sullivan did not have much more to contribute. Blackie and Frankie stood at almost the same time. Frankie spoke first.

"Thanks, Gabe. You've been a real help. I'm finally beginning to get a picture of who and what Karen Erikson was. There's a lot more legwork to do, but at least she'll look like a human being when I write about her in next Monday's paper."

After Sullivan had disappeared into the pressroom, Blackie turned to Frankie. "Like to have lunch? Maybe over at the Ramada Inn? There's something I'd like to show you, see what you think."

"Sure," she said, "why not?"

As they entered the coffee shop, Blackie took Frankie's arm in a proprietary manner. For a brief moment she thought, what the hell, the guy's so damned *nice;* but instead of releasing her after a few paces he began to use her elbow to guide her around the tables as if she were a half-blind twit. She angrily shook her arm free, and shot him a withering glance.

"Sorry!" he said exaggeratedly.

She shook her head. "You really *don't* understand, do you? Do you think I can't walk by myself? I'm forty-seven years old. Don't treat me like a high school girl."

"I can't believe you were *ever* a high school girl," he said with a grin.

She smiled somewhat sadly and replied, "Sometimes I don't think I ever was."

Seated at a small table directly in their path were Mayor Beaker Hogan and Winnie Taylor.

The mayor stood and gestured toward the two empty chairs. "Mrs. Mills, Chief Boone—join us for lunch. We were just about to order."

Blackie said, "Well, I do need to talk to you anyway, Beaker. You too, Winnie. Is it all right with you, Frankie?"

"Of course," she replied. "This is fine." She sat in the chair that Beaker Hogan had pulled out for her.

Winnie Taylor was wearing a particularly alluring costume of white, form-fitting jeans, and a pale blue, low-cut, sleeveless blouse. Her skin was tanned a dark, creamy brown; and Frankie, against her will, looked down at her own thin white arms and was repelled at the comparison. She suddenly felt very old and unattractive. She found herself wishing—absurdly, she knew—that the young woman would say something terribly naïve or stupid to counterweight such disgusting health and beauty.

But she was soon disappointed, for other than a cool detachment of manner, Winne Taylor conducted herself with a degree of poise and self-assurance that Frankie herself envied.

After the waitress departed Beaker Hogan asked, "What was it you needed from me, Blackie?"

"The will, Beaker," Blackie said. "When do you read the will? I'd like to be there."

"Too late," said Winnie. "Beaker brought the will out to Fairfield this morning. We've already gone over it."

"How was the estate divided?" Blackie asked.

Mayor Hogan turned toward Winnie, who nodded her approval.

"Equally," he said. "In three parts. A third to Jake, a third to Greg, and a third to Winnie . . . with Jake and I as co-executors."

"Was anything left to her brother, James Lan Franco?"

"No, no provision was made for him. But that's hardly surprising since, if anything, he's richer than Claudine was. I don't think she was concerned about his financial welfare."

"How about charities? The church—St. Andrew's Chapel? She was pretty wrapped up in that."

Beaker took a long slow sip of iced tea and replied, ". . . No, there was no provision made for any charities. I believe it was Claudine's intention to let her children decide for themselves which charities to support."

Frankie watched the mayor as he spoke, and received a very strong impression that he was lying. His eyes, which had been fixed firmly on Chief Boone's, shifted first to the table and then to Winnie, and then back to the table. His large head trembled, and sweat appeared around his hairline.

Two reporters approached the table, but Chief Boone restrained them with an upraised hand. "You're welcome to have your lunch, fellows," he said. "But no interviews until we've eaten. Okay?"

They agreed and went outside to wait.

"What a circus!" Winnie said.

"It can't be helped," said Frankie. "Your brother's a congressman—running for the Senate. There's no way to quiet this thing down."

"Mother was murdered, not Jake."

Frankie nodded. "True, but irrelevant."

Beaker Hogan reached for Winnie Taylor's hand. "Winnie and I are going to be married," he said. "Right away. Maybe this is a bad time to announce it, but maybe in a way it's a good time, too. People need each other when times are bad. We told Greg and Jake this morning."

"Congratulations," said Frankie. She looked at the mayor more carefully now: a former athlete, probably; still in reasonable condition; long, salt-and-pepper gray hair—certainly too long for his age, which she guessed to be somewhere in the mid-forties.

"This *is* a surprise," said Blackie.

"Beaker's going to run for Jake's old House seat," said Winnie. "Jake's promised to support him." She paused, and then asked, "Anything new in your investigation?"

"Nothing yet," Blackie replied, "except that we believe it was someone from around here who killed your mother."

Beaker and Winnie both leaned forward. "From around here?" said the mayor. "Are you sure? How do you know?"

"Several reasons. For one thing, he knew the road in and out of Fairfield. No drifter could've hid like he did. For another, we can't find any broken windows or locks out there. Looks like the guy had a key. Either that or Claudine left one of the doors open. Not impossible, but unlikely."

"A key!" Winnie exclaimed. "No one has the keys to Fairfield except us!"

"Us?" Frankie asked quietly.

"The family. Jake, Greg, me, Uncle Jim."

"What about you, Beaker?" asked Blackie. "Do you have keys to Fairfield?"

"Sure do. Claudine gave me a set a couple of years ago. But I must say, Blackie, your evidence seems kind of thin when you say the killer wasn't a transient. He could've scouted the place—got to know the roads. And who knows about the keys and open doors and such. Hell, he could've climbed in an open window!"

"True," said Blackie, "but I don't think so."

Winnie said, frowning, "Do you think someone in the family killed Mother? What exactly are you saying?"

"I'm not saying anything exactly," Blackie replied. "It's all very inexact at this point. But I'm not ruling out that possibility. There are a lot of unanswered questions."

"When you came in," said Winnie, "you mentioned that you needed to talk to me. What about? Do you think I murdered my own mother?"

Blackie shook his head and smiled. "You're jumping to conclusions. Don't be so defensive."

She asked, "What is it you need to know?"

"Where were you Sunday night?"

She didn't hesitate. "Out at the lake with Beaker—in his cabin. We spent the night together."

Beaker nodded slowly to confirm what she had said.

"What time did you—both of you—arrive at the lake?"

"Before dark," said Winnie. "Beaker was already there."

"Did either of you leave the cabin for any reason?"

"No," said Beaker, "we were together all night."

Once again Frankie sensed that the mayor was uncomfortable with his answer.

Blackie asked, "What time did you leave the cabin on Monday morning?"

"About seven, I guess," Beaker replied. "We had two cars. I went home for a while, and then to my law office, and later to City Hall."

Blackie turned to Winnie.

"I didn't leave at the same time. I went back inside the cabin and cleaned up some more. I left around eight or eight-thirty. I came here for breakfast. I must've got here about nine or so. That's when Charlie Swicegood told me about Mother's death."

"One more question," said Blackie. "Do you have the combination to your mother's safe?"

"Yes, I think so."

"Beaker?"

"I may have. In my own safe—with her other things."

After lunch the foursome left the coffee shop together and encountered the two reporters outside.

"Miss Taylor," one of the newsmen said immediately, "how're you holding up? How's Congressman Taylor holding up?"

"We're doing very well, thank you," she answered. "Life goes on. Mother always tried to teach us that no matter what happens you move on. You don't fall apart. Maybe you take second or third best, but you don't fall apart. Jake and Greg and I loved Mother, but we know she'd have wanted us to pick up the pieces and move on."

The same reporter, writing energetically, asked without looking up, "Chief Boone, do you have anything new to tell us?"

"Yes."

The reporter, who had expected a noncommittal answer, stopped writing abruptly and glanced quickly at his partner.

"We believe at this point," said Boone, "and we could be wrong, that Claudine Taylor's killer may be a local."

"A local," the second reporter said. "Do you mean—"

Blackie shrugged. "That's all I've got to say for now."

The first reporter asked hurriedly, "What about the priest? Anything new there?"

"No." Blackie shook his head. "Not yet. I will tell you this much though. There are some similarities in the two killings. Whether that pans out there's no way of telling yet."

"The same guy killed Claudine Taylor and the priest?"

"That's premature, but to be fair to you—it's a definite possibility. That's all for now. Would you two please inform the rest of the press? We'll go into it more later."

"Sure," the first reporter said.

Frankie smiled at Blackie's innocence. There is *no* way these two reporters would share anything with anyone. But so what? They were the ones who got the story. They deserved it.

When Beaker Hogan and Winnie Taylor had left, Frankie said, "Blackie, do you think Mayor Hogan told you the whole truth?"

"Hell, no. Winnie either for that matter."

Frankie said thoughtfully, "So she and the mayor are going to be married? That'll make him a very wealthy man."

"Very wealthy," said Blackie.

"Do you think something's wrong with the will?" Frankie asked.

"Can't say. By the way, would you like to come over to the office? I've still got something I'd like to show you." He patted his shirt pocket. "Then maybe you'd like to go on some interviews with me . . . strictly professional. The police chief and the owner of the *Kilkenny Weekly Times.*"

She nodded. "Bridie Embry first, right?"

"Right. I don't know why but I want to work the suicide first."

"Karen Erikson died first," said Frankie. "It seems appropriate."

9

THE pain returned as Frankie sat on the couch in Blackie's office waiting for him to attend to some administrative duties. She was glad that he had left her alone. She had no desire to listen to his clucking noises, and she knew that this pain, while not as severe as Monday's, was too strong to hide. It raced down her back and legs, forcing her to collapse forward until her face nearly touched her knees. She remained in that position for several minutes, taking in air in short, desperate gasps. She glanced up periodically at the door, hoping that Blackie would not return until she could regain control of herself. And then, as quickly as it had come, the needlelike pain vanished, leaving only a dull ache that made her feel as if she'd been hit in the back with a baseball bat. She resumed her normal posture just as Blackie reentered the room.

"Sorry to keep you waiting," he said. "People problems. Goes with the job."

She smiled and took a slow, deep breath to make certain that she would not be surprised by a sudden jolt of recurring pain.

"Coffee or tea?" he asked.

She shook her head. "What was it you wanted to show me?" She realized that her voice sounded impatient, so she added quietly, "You said you wanted my opinion on something."

He sat beside her on the couch and reached into his shirt

pocket. "Look at this. What do you make of it?" He handed her a small slip of paper containing several small, precisely written numbers.

"The combination of Claudine Taylor's safe?" she asked.

"Yes. The murderer left it behind. Study it carefully. Tell me what you think. And remember our original plot: He spots the safe in Claudine's closet, and then tortures her until she reveals the combination. Try to picture the scene in your mind."

Frankie turned her attention to the slip of paper. The writing was neat, ordered—accountantlike. She turned it over and looked at the reverse side. There was nothing written on the back. She lowered the paper to her lap and said, "What is it that bothers you, Blackie?"

"Think about it," he said. "Think about the whole scene."

She closed her eyes, but wasn't able to concentrate on the events at Fairfield. Her mind drifted to the residual pain in her back and to Dr. Ishikawa's office. "I don't see—"

"Have you ever scribbled a shopping list as you hurried into the grocery store?" he asked.

"Of course."

"What did it look like?"

"Dammit, Blackie, don't patronize me! What the hell are you—" Suddenly it was quite clear. She saw exactly what he was getting at, and she knew he was right. ". . . It's too neat, isn't it?"

"Right. This guy was supposedly in a hurry. He sticks a knife in Claudine's shoulders to get the combination . . . and he writes down the numbers with perfect symmetry, like a kid in school—like figures on a balance sheet. Not likely! If he'd written them then, under those conditions, the numbers would be askew, sloppy, or at the least—careless."

Frankie said slowly. "The combination was written *before* the killer got to the house! He brought it with him!"

"That's right. And that leads us to two other conclusions."

Frankie didn't ask what those two conclusions might be. She was getting irritated that his logic always seemed to be one step ahead of hers. She forced herself to concentrate and to anticipate his conclusions. "I see," she said, a small note of triumph in her voice. "The murderer *faked* the torture. He wanted to make it *appear* that he forced the combination out of her."

Blackie nodded. "Remember I said back at your office that it *looked* like she was tortured. The M.E.'s office couldn't give me a definite answer. . . . In my judgment the killer stabbed her in the shoulders *after* she was dead."

Frankie went on, "And that means he must've had a right to the combination. . . . Someone in the family, or someone Claudine had given the combination to."

"That's the way I see it."

"Then all we have to do is find out who had the combination. That ought to narrow it considerably." She was surprised by her use of the word *we* and she looked toward Blackie to see if he had reacted. But his face remained impassive.

He said, "The family . . . a few close friends maybe. It's beginning to come together a bit."

"What about the priest?" she said. "Was his torture real?"

"Can't say. One thing at a time."

Nothing about Bridie Embry correlated with Frankie's expectations. She had been certain, for example, that the old woman would live in a shuttered cottage with ivy crawling up the walls. And she had expected to find an active but stooped nonagenarian, probably wrapped in a fading, hand-knitted shawl.

But Bridie Embry would not cooperate with Frankie's preconceptions. The ivy-covered cottage turned out to be an ultramodern tract house on a fashionable cul-de-sac; and the stooped old lady proved to be ramrod-straight, clear-eyed, and dignified. She appeared at her door in a stylish, pale green dress. There was no shawl in sight.

"Mrs. Embry," Blackie said, "I'm Chief of Police Garner Boone and this is Francesca Mills—owner of the Kilkenny newspaper. We'd like to talk to you for a few minutes if we can." He spoke loudly, enunciating each word with the greatest of care.

"I know who you are," said Bridie Embry, ". . . both of you. Kilkenny is my home, too, you know. And it's not that big. And by the way, my hearing is quite good. You needn't shout."

"I'm sorry," said Blackie. "May we come in?"

"Please do." She smiled and Frankie thought that she had never seen so many creases, folds, and wrinkles. An ancient face—full of life—but very, very old.

"Mrs. Embry," Frankie began when they were seated, "we've come to ask you about Karen Erikson."

"Please call me Bridie," the old woman said. "I was called Mrs. Embry by my students for over sixty years, and frankly I got a little tired of hearing it. And besides, I never liked John Embry . . . a pompous windbag with slush for brains."

Frankie could see that Bridie Embry was not going to discuss Karen Erikson immediately, so she relaxed, sat back in her chair, and asked, "How long were you married, Bridie?"

"One year."

The answer seemed so incongruous that Frankie laughed out loud. But she stopped herself when she realized that there was nothing inherently humorous in the reply. She looked helplessly toward Blackie, who was grinning at her discomfort.

"You expected me to say forty or fifty years, didn't you?" said Bridie Embry, smiling pleasantly. "And that I've been a widow lo these many years."

"Something like that," Frankie admitted. "But to be honest, I don't think I'd better *expect* anything from you from now on. I think I'll just take each step as it comes."

"John Embry and I were divorced in 1912. It wasn't a popular thing back then. For quite a while I was considered a scarlet woman. But I've outlived all my critics. I've outlived *everyone* when you come right down to it—almost everyone, that is. There is one person who's still around from those old days: John Embry. Ninety-nine and still going strong. Lives in Dallas and writes me every Christmas—has for seventy years. Long letters, solves all the world's problems. I think the real reason he writes though is to make sure I know he's still alive. He refuses to die before I do."

This time Frankie laughed without apology, and Blackie joined in as well.

"So you want to know about Karen Erikson," Bridie Embry said with no prompting. "She was here on Saturday, you know. We talked about her mother, Grace. She died of consumption—tuberculosis they say nowadays—in 1936. Karen was sixteen—a beautiful child . . . and now—suicide." She spoke the word with a great sadness.

Blackie leaned forward and said, "Did she say anything that made you think she was about to kill herself?"

"No, I never got that impression at all, though I must say that she looked terrible. Her face was bloated and splotchy, and she had no figure at all. But it was her hair that depressed me the most. Thin, dirty, stringy. She used to have the loveliest hair in Gregg County. Long, gold, silky. And if there was a lovelier woman in this part of East Texas I don't know who it was—unless it was her mother. Grace was every bit as beautiful as Karen. I'll never forget the day they arrived in Kilkenny in 1930. Karen was still a girl but already stunning. When they stepped off the train the whole town caught its breath. What I remember most is their hats—identical black sombreros, tilted back on their heads. Their eyes shone out from under those hats like deep blue opals. Samuel Erikson was at the station that day. He watched them like a hungry old buzzard. I know because I watched him. He fell in love with Grace and courted her for six years—until she died. Then he went after Karen."

Frankie interrupted politely. "What else did Karen Erikson talk about when she was here Saturday?"

"Claudine Taylor. She said she'd seen Claudine. She'd invited Karen to Fairfield Saturday afternoon. Said she had something to tell her. Karen was going out there as soon as she left here."

Later, on the way to the patrol car, Frankie said to Blackie, "Divorced in 1912. Imagine that."

He laughed and took her arm.

Dr. Knox Presley lifted a dusty cardboard box onto his dining room table. He hadn't bothered to remove the white lace tablecloth, and a fine, dirty brown mist began to settle around the edges of the box. He realized what he had done and quickly snatched up the box and placed it on the floor. But he was too late. A grimy, rectangular stain was already embedded in the tablecloth.

"My wife will kill me," he said shamefully. He went into the kitchen and returned with a damp rag, and futilely began to scrub the stain. When it became obvious that he was only making matters worse, he tossed the rag aside and said, "Well, I've done about all the damage I can. She'll think I put the damn thing under the car while I changed the oil." He sighed, and then rolled back the tablecloth and placed the box back on the table.

Frankie winced as she watched him roughhouse the delicate linen. The stain that had at least been confined was now spread through the cloth. The man was uncommonly clumsy.

"Now let's look at those pictures," Dr. Presley said, fishing inside the box for a handful of photographs. "Hard to believe, three violent deaths: Sunday morning, Sunday night, and Monday morning. Kilkenny and Houston—the murder capitals of America." He paused and added peevishly, "Judge Moreno didn't need to send those bodies to Dallas. I could've done the autopsies." As he spoke he tried to remove a cluster of pictures from the box, only to have three-fourths of them slip from his fingers. He tried again with the same results, and finally thrust both hands into the box and withdrew a large assortment of photographs.

Frankie thought that it was a good thing the Dallas County Medical Examiner's office was handling the bodies. Dr. Presley looked as if he might be more comfortable with cough syrups and sprained ankles than with scalpels and dissections.

"Do you remember Karen Erikson yourself?" Blackie asked.

"No, I was only three when she left town. All I know is what my parents told me. That and these pictures." He spread out several faded black and white photographs on the table.

As she scanned them, Frankie could see that all of them featured a plump, smiling baby exclusively. Dr. Presley noticed this at the same time and laughed. "Only child . . . indulgent parents. Sorry." He scooped up the pictures, laid them aside, and reached back into the box.

The new ones heavily emphasized baby Knox, but in one he was being held by a very pretty young woman in shorts and a halter top.

"That's Karen Erikson," said Dr. Presley. ". . . I bought her some flowers this morning—even though her body's already gone to Dallas. *Somebody* had to remember her."

"Is this Samuel Erikson?" Blackie asked, pointing to a white-haired, sour-faced old man standing with his arm possessively around Karen.

"That's him. Pleasant-looking chap, eh?"

"What was he like?" Frankie asked. "What did your parents tell you about him?"

"They liked him. But then they liked everybody, so that's no indication of anything. They wouldn't even criticize Adolf Hitler. Mom said he must've had a difficult childhood."

"Did they tell you about the old man's death?" asked Blackie. "As we understand it, he was murdered."

"Yes. About six months before Karen left town. He was killed on the path to his office—beaten to death. Robbery, they said."

Frankie said to Blackie, "Gets to be a bit tiresome, doesn't it? Murder may not be as rare in Kilkenny as I'd imagined."

Blackie nodded. "I think murder is more common everywhere than any of us believe. Most murders are never solved—many are never even reported. I've heard it said that ten percent of all deaths might be murder in one form or another."

Frankie picked up another picture and said, "Is this James Lan Franco?" She indicated a tall, extremely handsome man apparently in his middle thirties. "I can see the resemblance."

Dr. Presley reached for the photograph. "Right. James Lan Franco. Good-looking devil, wasn't he? A real ladies' man." He laid Lan Franco's picture on the table and held up a larger one. "This is my mom and dad, standing beside Claudine and Curtis Taylor. Karen is kneeling beside me there in the front. Samuel must have taken the picture."

Frankie studied the photograph carefully. The Presleys were a very pleasant-looking couple—though a bit old (fortyish) to have such a young child. No doubt they doted on Knox—gave him everything. That was usually the case with older parents. They often submerged their own identities in what was now known as "parenting"—a dreadful word describing a dreadful concept. Claudine and Curtis Taylor appeared to be an average couple, though Claudine seemed very intense. Curtis was not distinctive in any way that Frankie could determine; that is, until she noticed his eyes. They were bright and alive, even in the old black and white photographs. Maybe intense was the wrong word to use to describe Claudine. Curtis, by virtue of his eyes, was intense. Claudine by contrast was merely nervous-looking. Karen, kneeling, was radiant, healthful. There was no doubt that she was beautiful, but it was an athletic, sensuous beauty—the innocent, perfectly formed country girl.

Blackie, who had been studying the photograph as well, looked up and, with a gesture that included all of the pictures they had seen, said, "Interesting . . . the rich get poor—or dead, and the poor get rich. Where did the Taylors and Lan Francos come from? How long had they been in Kilkenny at this time?"

"Miami, Oklahoma," Dr. Presley answered. "They came to town about 1940. They were all fast friends by the fall of

1941 when it all blew up—Samuel was killed and Karen left town."

"What about Beta Lan Franco?" Frankie asked. "Where was she during all this coziness? I know she and James were married at the time because they celebrated their golden anniversary this year—remember? That would mean they were married in 1933."

"Only one answer," said Dr. Presley. "James left her in Miami, Oklahoma, while he and his sister and brother-in-law came to Kilkenny. There was a lot of that going on in those late Depression years. Maybe Beta had a job and they didn't. People just didn't quit jobs in those days. Too hard to find new ones. He probably sent for her after they were established. Had to be after 1941. She's not in any of these pictures. Mom and Dad got to know her later, of course, but they never spoke of her in conjunction with the events before 1941."

"One more question, Knox," Blackie Boone said, "not about Karen Erikson. You were Claudine Taylor's physician. Did she give you the keys to Fairfield or the combination to her safe?"

"No. I seldom saw her at Fairfield. She always came to town to see me. As far as the safe is concerned, why in the world would she give me the combination to that?"

Frankie felt no inclination to discuss James Lan Franco's ornately carved front door, and she was glad to see that Blackie felt the same way. Neither spoke as they stood waiting for the massive door to open.

She used the time to mentally compose a side bar for the front page of next Monday's paper.

VIOLENCE IN THE LANGUAGE

Victim. The word has a frightening sound. It would be difficult, if not impossible, to think of a pleasant usage. It is not a word that is often used in Kilkenny, Texas. Of course, there is the odd

highway victim, or the drowning victim, or the
victim of disease; but these renderings do not
really convey the full violence resident in the
word. It needs a companion to properly shock the
reader; and recently in Kilkenny, we have been
subjected to just such a companion: murder.
Murder victim! And another: suicide. Suicide victim! The word takes on a new horror when cou-
pled with—

The door opened slowly and Beta Lan Franco appeared.
"Blackie, Mrs. Mills," she said. "How nice to see you. Please
come in."

She led them down the hallway toward the half-opened
door to the study. She knocked gently, leaned around the
opened door, and called out, "Jim, we have visitors: Chief
Boone and Francesca Mills—from the newspaper. Are you
decent?"

Frankie could hear no response, but Beta indicated that all
was well and that they should go in.

James Lan Franco was on his feet. "Blackie, good to see
you. Mrs. Mills, how are you?"

"I'm quite well, thank you," said Frankie, wondering how
grossly she was lying.

"We need to talk to you, and Beta too," Blackie said.

"We?" James said. "What does Mrs. Mills have to do with
Claudine's murder?"

"James," said Blackie, "wouldn't you rather read the truth
in our own newspaper than a pack of lies in *The Washington Post?* And this is not about Claudine—at least not directly. We need to talk to you about Karen Erikson. Her
suicide is a bit troubling, and we understand you knew her
years ago."

Beta Lan Franco frowned and wrung her hands nervously.

"Sure I knew her," James said. "But when you said 'years
ago' you weren't kidding! It was forty years ago—or more."
He paused and walked to the liquor cabinet. "Would either
of you like a drink?"

Frankie and Blackie both shook their heads. Beta lowered her eyes.

James poured himself a tall glass of bourbon and went on. "Maybe you know that Karen was here Saturday night."

"No," Blackie said. "We knew she saw Claudine, and Bridie Embry, but we didn't know she came here."

James scowled as if reproaching himself for revealing more than necessary. "She looked terrible," he said, taking a seat beside Frankie. "I couldn't believe it was her. Fat, bald, ugly. If it hadn't been for her eyes I wouldn't have recognized her at all. Dark blue—the same eyes."

"What did she want?" asked Blackie.

Frankie watched silently as James took a long slow drink of bourbon. He placed the glass on the table beside him, and then said, "She killed herself, didn't she! It's like I told Beta. Karen was probably making all the rounds before she took that acid. A last pilgrimmage. And she really wasn't *my* friend in the old days. She was *our* friend. Claudine's, Curtis's, Knox's folks', mine. We were *all* friends with Karen and Samuel." His voice was belligerent and Frankie wondered why. Blackie had asked a simple question—the same one she was about to ask. It didn't require an aggressive, defensive answer. But maybe James Lan Franco was simply an aggressive, defensive man.

Frankie looked toward Beta Lan Franco and asked, "Were you still in Oklahoma at that time, Mrs. Lan Franco? . . . I'm doing a story for the paper on Karen. I don't want to get the facts wrong."

Briefly Beta seemed to resent the question, but then she shrugged and said, "I stayed with my parents while Jim got a head start for us here. He sent for me during the war."

James said sharply, "Isn't that about enough ancient history, Blackie? What about my sister? What're you doing to catch Claudine's killer?" Before Blackie could answer, James looked toward Frankie and said, "As you know, I'm putting up a twenty-five-thousand-dollar reward. It's already been announced on the radio. Maybe you've heard?"

Frankie said that she hadn't heard.

"I'd like to put it in your newspaper," he said. "I'll be happy to pay for a full-page ad."

"That won't be necessary," she replied. "I'll carry the announcement as a public service." She wished that she could change the subject back to Karen Erikson, but she wasn't sure how to do so without assuming an authority she didn't possess. But such an assumption proved unnecessary, for Blackie brought the conversation back to the suicide.

"James, did you have any reason to think Karen Erikson might kill herself?"

"None—other than her looking so ragged, so ready to die. Like you said in the paper, Mrs. Mills: Maybe she just came home to do it."

"What did she say when she was here?" Frankie asked.

"Not much, just that she had seen Mrs. Embry and Claudine. Then we reminisced a little about the old days and she left. She was here—how long, Beta, an hour or so?"

Frankie turned to Beta Lan Franco. "Did you talk to Karen, too?"

"No, except at the door. I let her into the house. She visited Jim in the study. She left through the French doors." She motioned toward the rear of the study. "I didn't see her leave, but an hour is about right. Jim came out at eight o'clock."

Blackie said, "James, do you know why Karen Erikson left town forty years ago?"

"No. Samuel was killed. She left. That's all I know."

"Okay," said Blackie, "then let's talk about Claudine. Do you have the combination to her safe?"

"Of course. I've had it for years. Curtis and I put the damn thing in."

"Who else has the combination that you know of?"

"The kids—Jake, Greg, Winnie; I don't know, maybe Beaker Hogan. . . . That safe's been in a long time. The combination's never been changed."

"How about the keys to Fairfield? Do you have those?"

"Yes. And Claudine had the keys to our place. We *are* a family, after all!"

"Were you home Sunday night?"

"All night." James looked to Beta for confirmation. She nodded.

"Did you leave for any reason?" Blackie said slowly. He inadvertently motioned toward the French doors.

James's face reddened. "Are you suggesting that I slipped out and murdered my sister while my wife was asleep?"

"Of course not. I'm just trying to piece this puzzle together. Were you and Beta together the entire night?"

"No. Not if you're asking if we were like Siamese twins. I came in here to read—to be alone. I do *every* night. But I didn't leave the house."

Frankie asked smoothly, "Mr. Lan Franco, do you have any idea what the killer was looking for at Fairfield?"

"Money, I suppose. Jewelry. Anything of value."

"He tore up the whole house."

"So?"

"St. Andrew's Chapel was torn apart, too. Doesn't that strike you as quite a coincidence?"

"Yes, it does seem odd."

Blackie asked, "Do you know anything about Claudine's relationship with Father Stickney?"

"Just that she was one *hell* of a weird Catholic. Speaking in tongues, healing, agonizing—anything for a release of nerves. And she took it dead serious. You couldn't say a thing against Stickney."

Frankie started to ask whether Father Stickney had been Claudine's confidant, when she realized that of course he had been. Surely even charismatic Catholics exercised the confessional.

She considered the implications of such a relationship. With certainty there had been no secrets between the priest and Claudine Taylor. Was it something that they both *knew* that caused their deaths? If so, there must have been something tangible involved. No other explanation for the murderer's frantic searches made any sense. Did he find what he was looking for? Somehow, she doubted it. And where did Karen Erikson fit in? One thing was becoming more and more clear; all three deaths were integral parts of the solution to a central problem. She found that she liked playing detective. She wondered how carefully Blackie and his men had searched St. Andrew's Chapel.

But it was now well past the time when she must excuse herself and attend to the requirements of her urostomy. Dr. Ishikawa would be furious if he knew she'd waited this long. Already the heaviness was giving way to pain—though it was really more of an irritation at this point. She could use the Lan Francos' facilities or explain that she was growing tired and would like to go home. She chose the latter.

"Sure," said Blackie. "Let's go now. You do look a bit peaked. And here I've been dragging you all around town."

"It's been interesting," she said. "I'll have background for the *Weekly Times* that the national papers won't come close to."

Beta and James both walked them to the door.

"I'll bring over the details on that twenty-five-thousand-dollar reward in a day or two," James said.

"That'll be fine."

In the car Blackie said, "Want to have dinner later? Maybe at the lake?"

"No, thanks. I appreciate the offer but I've got other plans."

10

THE night was warm and very dark; and as Frankie left her house to begin her detective work, she reached into the glove compartment of her car to make certain the flashlight was still there. She placed it on the seat beside her and drove to St. Andrew's Chapel.

Even though the car was two years old, the dashboard clock was still working—something of a minor miracle, she thought. Nine-thirty. She had left Blackie Boone at a little past five. Had it really taken her over four hours to take care of her personal needs, fix a bit of supper, and change clothes? She was getting slow, that's all there was to it. She laughed as she remembered how she used to criticize her mother for moving so slowly. If she could see her mother now, she would admit that finally, after all these years, she understood.

She was glad she had decided to venture out on her own. She was tired of standing in the shadows while Blackie took the lead. And though she was beginning to appreciate that he wasn't quite the bumpkin she had imagined, she still had no wish to extend their relationship in the direction he obviously desired. And besides, how romantic would he feel if he found out that she urinated through her side?

As she had suspected, the door to St. Andrew's Chapel was open. It wouldn't have been like the local Catholics, however atypical, to discourage worshippers, even at nine-thirty on a Tuesday night. But if the door had been locked, she had been prepared to climb in a window if necessary. She was determined to get in and look around. *Something* tied together the deaths of Claudine Taylor and Father Stickney, and probably Karen Erikson, too. There were too many connecting threads for it to be otherwise. Maybe that something was inside. She wished she could search Fairfield as well; but with the three Taylor children taking up temporary residence there, that would be impossible.

She didn't feel arrogantly that she could accomplish what the police couldn't. It wasn't that at all. It was more a question of a starting point, an issue, a focus. Even if she didn't find a thing, the adventure might help her to begin thinking clearly about the deaths. And she had to admit that it would be quite a coup for a one-horse weekly newspaper to scoop the big boys on this story; even if it only meant pointing the authorities in the proper direction.

The flashlight proved unnecessary, for someone had left a dim light burning behind the altar.

The chapel walls were lined with religious paintings, most of which emphasized glossolalia or healing or some other aspect of the miraculous. The statuary reflected the same bias, as did the two large stained-glass windows that rose above the loft.

Frankie moved slowly down the center aisle toward the front. She wondered what kind of man Father Robert Stickney had been. What kind of pressures or influences would cause a man who had been immersed in the traditions of order and ritual to chuck them aside and lead his followers into disorder and intemperance?

She stopped near the altar and turned to survey the room from a new perspective. The paintings on the walls were hung two, three, and four high, the top two rows virtually out of viewing range. But she guessed there was nowhere else to hang them, since every square foot of space, including the ceiling (which featured cherubs with harps and bows cavorting with winged serpents in a background of clouds and sky), was in use. A rolling ladder was stationed awkwardly near the halfway point on the chapel wall and

Frankie wondered why it had not been pushed back to its position at the rear. But the priest's murder had no doubt left the congregation in disarray, and no one had thought to attend to such matters.

There was no sense searching the usual places. The police, and the killer, too, had certainly done that. Drawers, and cabinets and closets, and pockets and cases would be a waste of time. She looked toward the door to Father Stickney's study. Searching in there would not be productive either. The murder had been committed in the study and the room had been literally torn apart. The chapel itself seemed to be the most logical—

She suddenly interrupted her line of thought. There was a noise coming from the study. A drawer opening, a footstep, a cough. She couldn't be sure. But one thing was certain: she was not alone!

She experienced an immediate shortness of breath. Had the murderer returned to complete his search? If so, she had better get out of the church, and at once! She had no desire to be added to his list of victims.

She began to creep toward the outer door, and then hesitated. What if she could somehow catch a glimpse of whoever was in the study? She could break the case wide open. If she left now, by the time she got back with help, it might be too late. The intruder would surely be gone. Maybe if she threw open the study door she could see who was inside and then slam the door shut before he could grab her. But could she make it to her car before he caught up to her? Probably not. He would have to be very slow indeed not to overtake *her.* She ran like an aging giraffe. She ridiculed herself for even considering such a foolhardy plan.

At that moment the door to the study flew open and a dark figure swept into the chapel. Frankie's breath left her entirely. She gasped for air and began to faint toward the altar.

She thought crazily as she fell that at least she would die, Becket-like, in church.

But strong arms caught her before she hit the hard oak

altar, and a gentle voice said reassuringly, "I've got you. Don't worry, you'll be fine! Just relax now. I'm going to lay you down on the rug."

She felt her head clearing, and she opened her eyes to see a concerned middle-aged face staring down at her.

"Who—" she began, but the man restrained her by passing his index finger over her lips. "Don't talk, not yet," he said. "Just relax. I've frightened you, I'm afraid. I'm terribly sorry. I heard a noise out here, and with Father Stickney's murder and all, I burst out like a thoughtless fool to see what was going on. I must've terrified you."

She nodded weakly.

He raised her head and held it above the level of her body. "You'll be fine now. Let the blood circulate for a bit."

"Who are you?" she asked.

"I'm Bishop Benjamin Foster. St. Andrew's Chapel is part of my diocese. I'm trying to make some sense out of what's happened here."

She put her hand on his arm to indicate that she was all right now, and he removed his hand from under her head. She rose on one elbow.

"What were you doing in the study?" she said.

"What were *you* doing out here? Are you a Catholic? And who are you anyway?"

She sat up. "I'm Francesca Mills." She held out her hand awkwardly. "I own the Kilkenny newspaper. No, I'm not a Catholic. I wasn't here to worship. Like you, I came here to try to make some sense out of Father Stickney's murder."

He shook her hand, and then used it to pull her slowly to her feet.

"I think I understand," he said. "You heard me in the study and thought I might be the killer returned to the scene of the crime. When I charged out you panicked."

"Something like that."

"What were you looking for?" he asked.

"I'm not sure. Maybe the same thing the killer was. The study was torn apart, you know. Maybe just a thief looking

for money, I don't know. But somehow I don't think so. And
we've had two other deaths recently also."

"Claudine Taylor and Karen Erikson."

"Yes. And they seem to be tied together. As to Father
Stickney, I don't know. But he *was* her pastor. They were
very close."

"A triple murder? Did the Erikson woman really kill herself?"

"That seems to be the case."

The priest frowned and rubbed his chin with his cupped
hand. "What the hell's going on in this little town? . . . I
knew we were heading for trouble when I allowed this mis-
guided passion to bloom here. But I thought it better to
confine them to one place than to have them leaven other
East Texas congregations. I guess I was wrong. This charismatic apostasy seems to have exploded in my face."

"I don't think it has anything to do with religion, Bishop
Foster."

"You think not? You'd be surprised how everything
comes back to religion in the end."

She nodded abstractly. "Maybe so. . . . What's happening
here? I don't understand."

"The same thing that's happening all across the country—
the world, for that matter: the worship of emotions. Men
and women can't face reality and they succumb to hysteria."

"Hysteria is a strong word."

"Not strong enough perhaps. These people *abuse* the
scriptures. They *use* them, deliberately misconceiving certain passages. Wherever this movement raises its ugly head
you find confusion, obscurity—a lack of knowledge and reason. Ironically, the Catholic involvement began at an institution that should've known better—Duquesne University in
Pittsburgh . . . sixteen, maybe seventeen years ago. Those
clowns didn't know what they were starting. Now it's spread
like a cancer. Unstoppable. Damned nonsense! But what to
do about it, that's the paradox. *Whatever* I decide leads to
problems. And now . . . murder."

"I can appreciate your theological difficulties, Bishop Foster, but I think our murders are much less intricate. When we finally get the rock turned over I'm sure the same old motives will crawl out: greed, envy, fear of exposure—lust for power. There's not much variety, I'm afraid. I'm sure that murder for doctrinal disputes ended with the Inquisition."

"Well, you're wrong about that. Every day you read about murderers who justify their crimes by invoking God's name. And mothers cutting the hearts out of their babies to exorcise demons. And human sacrifices in the California desert. I'm afraid you underestimate the infinite corruptibility of the religious impulse in man, Mrs.—is it Mrs.?—Mills."

"Yes, it's Mrs. I'm divorced." She could see that this conversation would lead to a dead end, so she asked, "How well did you know Father Stickney?"

"Not well at all. I stayed away as much as possible."

"Did he have any personal quirks? I mean apart from this charismatic thing?"

"Not that I know of. A pretty normal guy otherwise. A *nice* guy. A bit absentminded."

"Did he keep a calendar or a journal or something like that?"

"No. That would be helpful, wouldn't it?"

She nodded. "The police would have it anyway. It was just a thought."

"Wait a minute," the bishop said. "I did find something—it fell out of the sleeve of his suit—a note, a reminder. I stuck it in the desk drawer. Come on, let's go have a look." He led her into the study. "Here it is," he said, holding up a small piece of paper:

C. called. Finish sermon, then go see her—
tonight.

Frankie took the note in her hand, looked it over, and said, "Not much, is it? What's it tell us? 'C' could stand for Claudine Taylor. But no date."

"I'd say it was written on a Saturday night," said Bishop

Foster. "Stickney was still working on his Sunday sermon, and he had a sense of urgency about finishing it. And he wouldn't refer to one of his weekday or Saturday homilies as a 'sermon.' Since Vatican II we're supposed to use the term *homily* at all times, but some of us still say 'sermon' for Sunday Mass. No, this was written on a Saturday night. And I'd say it was this past Saturday night."

"How do you figure that?"

"Well, the suit was in the dirty-clothes hamper on top of a red chasuble. Last Saturday, June eleventh, was the Feast of Saint Barnabas, which we generally celebrate in my diocese. Stickney would've worn the red chasuble for Saturday morning Mass to recognize the martyr. Since the suit, with the note in the sleeve, was on top, it had to have been tossed into the hamper after last Saturday morning's Mass. Probably when he went to bed Saturday night. Or maybe he changed suits before he went out to Fairfield. Perfectly logical, eh?"

"You're quite a detective, Bishop Foster."

He laughed. "Assuming the note and the suit and the chasuble hadn't been there since the last martyr's feast."

"That's possible," said Frankie. "But I think you've got it right. Now, what does it *mean?*"

11

A T eleven o'clock Wednesday morning, Frankie sat in Blackie Boone's office listening to a veteran pathologist from the Dallas County Medical Examiner's office. The report was dry, and the delivery bored. It was obvious that the man was unimpressed by death in any multiples. He could well be giving the morning weather, she thought.

"Carbolic acid . . . phenol, is devastating to human tissue," the doctor droned on. "That's one of the reasons why its use as an antiseptic has declined over the years. When the Erikson woman swallowed the phenol, her esophagus was maimed to such an extent that any undue pressure would cause it to rupture. We believe that either voluntarily or involuntarily she began to vomit. This strain ripped open the esophagus, resulting in massive hemorrhaging, severe shock—perhaps a short comatose period—and death."

"Why would she choose such a terrible way to kill herself?" Frankie asked.

The pathologist shook his head. "Hard to say. The pain must have been agonizing. Some suicides are very conscious of impending pain, some couldn't care less."

Blackie asked, "You said on the phone that there was no reason to suspect anything other than suicide. Do you still feel that way?"

"Yes. No signs of a struggle, no extraneous wounds. Not

to mention that it's just too weird to think that someone would commit murder by forced ingestion of carbolic acid."

"This town has been nothing if not weird lately," said Frankie, a smile curling cynically at the corner of her mouth.

The assistant medical examiner went on. "If you want my opinion, I'll give it." He paused, and it was apparent that his opinion was coming whether or not it was desired. "I think Karen Erikson killed herself all right. And I think she deliberately *chose* the most horrible method she could think of. She *wanted* the pain!"

"What possible evidence can you have for such an opinion?" said Blackie.

"Thirty years' experience. Invariably, whenever particularly ghastly suicides come along, I find that the victims wanted it that way. Needed it that way. Something happened, some shock, some surprise, some realization, something unbearable. They needed to blast that something from their minds—as violently as possible. I think you'll find that your poor old suicide recently came into contact with *something*—emotional, physical, mental . . . something she couldn't handle. It may have just been a sudden insight into her wasted life. . . . But she needed to go out screaming."

Frankie winced at his vivid remarks, but she found herself nodding.

The pathologist opened another folder. "The priest . . . not many surprises there. The shotgun blast killed him, that's certain. Tore off his left arm and destroyed his carotid artery. The external and internal jugular veins were severed as well, and several pellets were even found in his brain, though these had no relation to his death. Instant loss of all the body's blood. Shock. Hopeless from the beginning. Like a slaughtered steer." He recoiled at his own words and said, "Sorry, I'll try to be more professional. Too many years of this and you begin to forget you're cutting up human beings."

"Was Stickney being tortured?" Blackie asked. "Was the killer aiming for the arm?"

The pathologist shrugged. "You suggested as much on the phone, Chief Boone. How can I answer you? I don't know how good a shot the murderer was."

Blackie answered his own question. "It'd take a pretty piss-pot poor shot to miss that much from point-blank range."

"What about the times of the deaths?" asked Frankie.

"No problem on the priest, of course," Blackie cut in. "He finished Monday morning Mass at eight, visited with members of his congregation for fifteen minutes or so, and his body was discovered at nine. Forty-five minutes. I'm sure the M.E.'s office couldn't pinpoint it any closer than that."

"That's correct," the pathologist said. "The same with Claudine Taylor. Your evidence narrows the time of her death from her telephone call to your station at eleven P.M. Sunday night until your man, Swicegood, found her body at about eleven-twenty. Close enough. The Erikson woman, however, presents a more difficult problem. She was apparently in her room alone for a considerable period of time. Her body was discovered Sunday afternoon just before three. Dr. Presley was on the scene shortly thereafter, and from his preliminary report we know that rigor mortis had just begun to stiffen the muscles around her eyes. Four hours . . . six hours. Maybe ten, eleven o'clock Sunday morning. No closer than that."

He reached for a third folder. "Now, regarding Claudine Taylor. There was a great deal of blood lost from the knife wounds to her shoulders, but we don't believe she bled to death. As you suspected, Chief Boone, the cause of death was a broken neck—specifically, a crushed trachea. Life was untenable after that."

Blackie asked, "Have you been able to determine whether she was stabbed before or after she died?"

"No. And we considered both of your telephone calls on that matter. The first time you called you suggested torture, and we haven't come up with any forensic evidence to confirm or deny that theory. When you called back you suggested faked torture—that she was stabbed after death; and we can't make a definitive determination on that either. The broken neck and the stabbing simply occurred too close together. If the killer had waited an hour or so between attacks, we could tell you for sure. But as it is, no such luck."

Blackie frowned. "It's never easy," he said.

Frankie felt guilty as she watched the disappointment register on Blackie's face. She should have told him about her visit to St. Andrew's Chapel and her conversation with Bishop Foster. Maybe it wasn't important, but it *was* information; and he had certainly kept her informed. She didn't know why she had been so secretive, other than a small-minded resentment for his not fitting the mold she had previously fashioned for him; and, of course, there was her desire to contribute to the investigation on her own and not as a sounding board for his ideas. But there was no excuse for her self-centeredness, and as soon as the pathologist left she would tell Blackie everything.

While the two men continued their discussion on the more mundane aspects of the autopsies, Frankie allowed her mind to drift to her morning visit to the Tyler Diagnostic Clinic. It had seemed uneventful—muscle tissue and bowel samples, a short visit with Dr. Ishikawa. But afterward, as she drove back to Kilkenny, she wondered if she might have reason to hope. The pain hadn't recurred since yesterday afternoon in Blackie's office—other than the mild irritation she'd felt at the Lan Francos'. And Dr. Ishikawa hadn't seemed particularly alarmed, as he might have if the previous tests had revealed anything ominous. Of course, using the dispassionate internist as a benchmark could be very silly indeed. He was not likely to tremble with alarm even if he was convinced that her cancer had returned. But nevertheless, she had felt hopeful, and she encouraged the feeling now.

When the assistant medical examiner had gone, Frankie turned to Blackie to bring him up to date on her activities. But before she could begin, Jake Taylor and his campaign manager Edgar Brooks came into the office.

"Jake, Edgar, thanks for coming," said Blackie.

Frankie smiled her greetings and accepted Edgar Brooks's handshake.

"Coffee or tea, anyone?" asked Blackie.

The two men ordered coffee, and Frankie tea. Blackie stuck his head out the door and gave their orders to Officer Bobby Ridgeway, who scurried toward the front.

"Let's make ourselves comfortable," Blackie said, taking a seat on the couch and indicating by patting the spot next to him that Jake should join him. Edgar Brooks and Frankie sat in the two remaining chairs.

"Anything new?" said Jake. "It's been three days now. Winnie tells us you suspect that a local killed Mother. Any idea who?"

"No, none. Not yet. I'm working on it."

". . . Blackie," Jake began hesitatingly, "have you considered bringing in the FBI? It shouldn't be too difficult to find a pretext for calling them in. Presumed flight over the state line . . . government secrets, something like that. After all, she was *my* mother. We could say the guy might have thought that her safe contained top-secret stuff. Now, I'm not trying to insult you, but this type of case may be beyond your limitations—I mean the limitations of your office."

Edgar Brooks continued the thought. "The director himself called me—at the President's suggestion. The pretext will be just a formality. The FBI will step in the minute you request them."

It seemed to Frankie from the inflection in the fat little campaign manager's voice that he was less enthusiastic about the idea of bringing in the FBI than Jake Taylor, and that if it hadn't been for the director's call he would never have counseled such a move.

Edgar confirmed her impression by nervously crossing and uncrossing his short legs and adding, "Of course, sometimes outside influences only muddy up the waters and confuse everyone. And worse, they leak negative information to the press. It's a way of life with them. We've got to be as careful as we can with your image, Jake." He turned to

Blackie. "But they'll help if you need them, Chief. They've made their offer clear."

It was a suggestion easily refused, thought Frankie—squelched at the outset by Edgar's lackluster support. Why did he not want the FBI in on the case? What did he care? Leaks to the press? Nonsense. Everyone knew that the FBI was the *least* talkative of law enforcement agencies. She'd certainly spent enough years trying to shake loose information from them. She shrugged. Maybe it was just a matter of Edgar's desire to protect his own sphere of influence. Federal authorities tended to disturb matters. Big fish in a small pond.

Blackie smiled pleasantly. "I've had no shortage of offers of help. Believe it or not, even Army Intelligence called me this morning. Some guy in Killeen . . . Fort Hood. Sounded like he didn't have anything better to do. Said he'd be happy to drive up and help me. Apparently pretexts are no problem for the Army either."

"Well, think it over," Jake said. "Don't be too proud. The FBI knows what it's doing. And I want Mother's murderer run to ground. I'm glad we've got capital punishment back. I'd like to squeeze that syringe myself!"

Frankie asked, "Congressman Taylor, have you heard from your Democratic opponent? We have his public statements of condolence, of course. But I wonder if he's called you personally. Our readers would be interested to know."

"No, he hasn't called me. . . . Can I speak off the record?"

She nodded.

"He's a first-class asshole. Edgar tells me the Democrats are frantically trying to find a way to use Mother's death to their advantage. Despicable bastards!"

Frankie made some notes, and said as she wrote, "I'm not quoting you, Congressman. Just jotting down some general thoughts on campaigns and party politics."

"They really want this Senate seat," said Edgar Brooks. "They'd do anything to get it. Anything! But they're not going to win. They'd like to go back to a one-party state, but those days are gone. Jake Taylor will serve in the Senate for the next thirty years. He's still a young man, you know."

Frankie put her pen down and said good-naturedly, "Relax, Edgar, my newspaper is a small-town weekly."

The campaign manager frowned momentarily, then laughed, and the others joined in. "Habit," he said. "Sorry."

"Jake," said Blackie, "the reason I asked you two here today is because I need to ask you both some questions. Let me make it clear that you aren't being singled out for special treatment—bad or good. I need answers from everyone. I need a clear picture of what's happened since Saturday. I'm sure you both understand."

"Of course," Edgar replied.

"Good. Then let's begin with Saturday. Were you two together?"

Jake nodded. "All day. Dallas, Plano, Irving. Politics, planning, campaigning—all day. Preliminaries. We haven't begun in earnest yet."

"Lining up support," said Edgar, nodding vigorously.

Officer Ridgeway appeared at the door with the coffee and tea, and reluctantly entered and began to serve. He accomplished his task and disappeared instantly.

"Saturday night?" asked Blackie.

"We returned to Longview, to Edgar's house," Jake explained. "We slept very late Sunday morning. That's why we were out so late Sunday night . . . when you were trying to get ahold of me to tell me about Mother."

"Where did you go Sunday night?"

Edgar answered for him. "Several different places. Dinner at Will Stone's. Great fish. Drinks at Barney's, and on to the country club."

"Can all of this be verified?"

"Sure," said Edgar.

"Were you together the entire night, from dinner until we reached you?"

"Yes," Jake replied. "Talked politics until it ran out our ears. One nice thing about being single is that neither one of us has to report in to anyone. Who would've thought Mother would be murdered that night?"

"What about Monday morning? After you two left my office, where did you go?"

"Back to Longview first," Jake said. "I took Edgar home. But I wouldn't have been able to sleep, of course, and there was no sense driving back to my place in Plano; so from Edgar's, I drove straight out to Fairfield."

"What time did you get there?"

"Oh, I don't know—seven-thirty or so. Why?"

"Well, frankly, because Father Stickney was killed Monday morning. Was there anyone at Fairfield when you arrived? Judge Moreno, Dr. Presley?"

"No. It was deserted. Everyone had gone home. Mother's body was already at Marsh's."

"So no one can verify that you arrived at Fairfield at seven-thirty?"

"No. Uncle Jim, Greg, and Winnie came in the afternoon."

Blackie turned to Edgar Brooks.

"I went straight to bed," the campaign manager said. "Slept until one or two. And the *President* called me Monday evening."

Jake said, "*I* received a call from the President Monday afternoon, around two. I called Edgar around three."

Blackie asked, "Jake, do you have the combination to your mother's safe?"

"Yes, it's in my papers somewhere."

"And naturally you have the keys to Fairfield."

"I got in, didn't I?"

Blackie turned to Edgar. "Do you have either the combination or the keys?"

"Me? Well, no. But I guess technically yes. You know, I keep most of Jake's papers and extra keys and things. I suppose they're in there somewhere. What's this all about?"

"Nothing special," said Blackie. "I'm asking everyone the same questions. May I ask why you keep Jake's personal items?"

"You must realize I'm his executive assistant as well as his campaign manager. *He's* too busy to bother with paperwork and errands. I see that he stays organized and that things get done—you know, personal or otherwise."

After Jake Taylor and Edgar Brooks had left, Frankie finally found the opportunity to tell Blackie about her visit to St. Andrew's Chapel. To her surprise he threw back his head and roared, explaining that Bishop Foster had already told him all about it, including the fainting episode. "Did you think you'd flushed the killer?" he teased. "The *investigative* reporter. Kilkenny's own Nellie Bly."

She was not amused, and she resolved angrily that she would not worry about keeping him informed in the future.

He saw that he had gone too far, and tried to make amends by inviting her to lunch; but she told him what he could do with his lunch, tossed in some suggestions about the heritage of his Lufkin ancestors, and stormed from his office.

Edgar Brooks and Jake Taylor stood on the curb outside City Hall.

Jake Taylor put his arm around his aide and said, "Edgar, I really appreciate you covering for me. I'd've had a hard time explaining where I really was Sunday night. Do you think the story will hold up?"

"Oh, sure, sure. No question about it. The boys at the country club will back us all the way. Will Stone's in our hip pocket, and I got the guys at Barney's believing you were really there that night. But do me a favor, will you?"

"What's that, Edgar?"

"Stay away from married women, okay? At least until after the election."

12

THE Kilkenny City Hall was erected in 1883 in the center of the town square, and remained pretty much as built through its first hundred years. It had been renovated several times, of course, but the basic structure was the same. A forward-looking architect had disregarded the gaudy conventions of his day and had designed a clean, simple, functional building that no one since had found any need to improve on. The walls were granite and limestone, and the roof heavy Spanish tile. There was every indication that the building would last another hundred years.

The edifice was, in fact, one of the reasons Frankie had decided to come to Kilkenny. Any town that had the good sense to preserve such a graceful structure couldn't be all bad.

She was irritated, to be sure, at Blackie Boone's patronizing attitude; however, as she rushed out of his City Hall office, she was not too angry to pause once again and admire the simple beauty and symmetry of the building.

She then continued on across the square to the office of the *Kilkenny Weekly Times.*

Gabe Sullivan greeted her with startling news: "James Lan Franco's been taken to the hospital. About four hours ago. I talked to one of the servants."

"What is it?" Frankie asked quickly.

"No idea. I do know, though, that his legs were puffed up so bad he couldn't walk."

"Thanks, Gabe," she said, turning back toward the door. As an afterthought she added, "Where, Gabe? *Our* hospital?"

"Right."

Curtis Taylor Memorial Hospital was located on a side street just off the square, and Frankie reached it in a matter of minutes.

Blackie Boone was already standing in the lobby when she walked in. He said, "You've heard, eh?"

"Gabe just told me. What is it? How is he?"

"I just got here, but I did talk to Knox Presley. James'll be all right—at least for now."

Dr. Presley approached and Blackie said, "Here, I'll let Knox tell you himself."

"James Lan Franco's going to be all right?" Frankie asked.

Dr. Presley shrugged. "That's hard to say. He won't die today if that's what you mean—at least I don't think so. But I can't speak for next month, or even next week."

"What's wrong with him?"

"Classic case of cirrhosis. Far advanced from the looks of it. A fifth of bourbon a day for forty years—and lately even more. Body can't take it. I'd guess his liver is totally wasted, shrunk to half its normal size."

Frankie nodded. She remembered the spider veins in Lan Franco's face, and his beet-red color. She shouldn't have been surprised.

"Yellow nodules around the eyes," Dr. Presley went on, "and the jaundice will spread before this episode's over."

"Can we see him?" asked Frankie.

"I don't see why not. His nephew Greg is in with him now. But that shouldn't matter."

They walked across the lobby and down a short hallway. Dr. Presley led them through an open door, but instead of the usual adjustable bed and other hospital apparatus, the room contained a couch and several overstuffed chairs.

"Sitting room," said the doctor. "This is James Lan Franco's *suite.*" He spoke the last word with a mild disdain.

"Doesn't matter that the hospital's filled. They had this room cleared out in ten minutes. Don't know where they tossed the poor bastard who was in here."

They entered the second room through the connecting door, and Dr. Presley said, "How you feeling, James?"

James Lan Franco, who was lying on the bed in a standard hospital gown with his hands behind his head and with the blankets cast down around his feet, replied softly, "Only fair, Knox, only fair." When he saw that Frankie was present, he reached for the blankets and pulled them up to his chest.

"Rotten luck," Blackie said.

"Luck, hell," James answered bitterly, his voice still soft. "It was the booze. I always knew this would happen. Just wouldn't admit it to myself."

Greg Taylor said, "Aunt Beta went to get some more of Uncle Jim's things. She'll be back before long. Some week. First Mother, then this."

"I'm not dead yet," said James, obviously trying to sound cheerful. "Don't bury me while I'm still alive." His voice diminished as he talked, and the cheerfulness gave way to distress.

Frankie said, "You *look* well."

No one in the room responded, including James Lan Franco, because all knew that her statement was clearly false. Even Frankie could not make herself follow up on the comment, except to say, "You'll be looking better soon."

Winnie Taylor and Mayor Beaker Hogan entered the room together, followed by Jake Taylor and Edgar Brooks.

"Dammit, Uncle Jim," Jake Taylor said, "what's this all about?"

James smiled. "I'm afraid I'll never see you sworn in as a senator."

"Nonsense," said Jake. "You'll outlive us all. We've always known that. Not that you deserve it." He forced a chuckle.

Winnie Taylor stepped forward and asked pointedly, "What's wrong with you, Uncle Jim?"

"Liver . . . shot to hell. Apparently I've knocked out all the good cells and replaced them with crap."

"The tests aren't all complete yet," Dr. Presley protested. But his voice betrayed him, and everyone knew that the tests were complete enough.

At that point Beta Lan Franco marched angrily into the room and exclaimed, "Good God! What is this, a convention? Knox, get these people out of here. Jim needs rest. You know that."

Dr. Presley nodded guiltily. "Of course. You're right, Beta. Come on, let's all get out. It's gotten out of hand."

Frankie backed out of the door first. Of all who were present, she felt she was the least qualified to impose. Edgar Brooks, Beaker Hogan, and Blackie Boone joined her in the sitting room. Dr. Presley came out next and said, "The family's staying a few minutes longer."

"Sad," said Blackie. "They're dying off."

"All families die off," said Frankie. "Or haven't you noticed?"

"I guess you're right," he replied, shaking his head.

Dr. Presley said, "Alcohol's a killer. If people could only see what it does to their insides. And yet I drink myself, so there you are."

Greg Taylor was the first member of the family to exit the inner room, and Blackie Boone took him by the arm and said, "Greg, can I talk to you for a minute? While the others are inside?"

"They'll be right out," said Greg.

"Just a few questions."

"Okay, fine."

Frankie moved closer and tried to appear unobtrusive.

"Did you and your mother get along?" Blackie asked.

"No."

"Why not?"

"She refused to understand what's important to me."

"And what's that?"

"The survival of the planet. Of all of us. And other things. Lots of other things. She just couldn't believe that I had concerns other than religion or the Taylor money."

"Were there arguments?"

"Sure—lots of them."

"Violent?"

"Never, I'm not a violent person."

"Over money?"

"Well, yes. But not the way you make it sound. I'm not interested in money as such . . . only in the good it can do. The peace it can bring."

Blackie smiled pleasantly. "I've never found that it brings much peace, son. But that's beside the point. . . . Do you have the combination of your mother's safe?"

Greg nodded slowly. "Sure," he said. "But there was never any significant amount of money in it, if that's what you mean."

"No, not that," said Blackie. "You have the keys to Fairfield, don't you?"

"Yes." He began to withdraw a large key ring from his pocket, but Blackie held up a palm to indicate that it wasn't necessary.

Jake and Winnie Taylor came out of the room next, and Jake said, "Beta's staying. She'll sit by his bed while he sleeps."

Winnie said, "I think he got yellower while we were in there."

Beaker Hogan put his arm around her and said, "Come on, Win, let's walk over to my office. We can come back later."

Edgar Brooks said to Jake Taylor, "I think it'd be better if we didn't emphasize this to the reporters. They're thinning out anyway. But you know how it is—cirrhosis means liquor in the family. That could lose you a lot of Baptist votes. . . . We won't cover up anything. But let's try to keep it low-key."

Jake nodded and they walked out into the hall.

Dr. Presley left at the same time to perform his hospital rounds.

Greg Taylor started to follow, but Blackie said, "Hold on a minute, Greg. One other thing."

"What?"

"Where were you Sunday night?"

". . . Home, no. I went to a meeting in Tyler. Nuclear freeze."

"Can you back that up?"

"Certainly."

"What time did you get home?"

"I'm not sure. Midnight or one o'clock. I was home when you called about Mother's murder. About two in the morning, wasn't it?"

"Right. Were you alone when I called?"

"Yes."

"Where were you Saturday night?"

"What's Saturday got to do with anything?"

"Please."

"Home—all night. And no, I can't back it up."

"Monday morning?"

"After I left your office, I went back home. I told Charlie Swicegood I was going home. And Winnie came by at nine-thirty or so."

Blackie said, "Thanks, Greg. That's all. You can go now. Sorry about your uncle."

When the young man had disappeared down the hall, Frankie said, "Remarkably stuffy for a kid his age, wouldn't you say?"

Blackie laughed. "Nice enough, I suppose. He just doesn't think any of the rest of us has any sense."

"Maybe we don't," said Frankie. "Maybe we don't."

County Precinct Judge Susan Moreno entered the hospital lobby through the front door at the same time that Frankie and Blackie came out of the hallway.

"Chief Boone," Judge Moreno called out, "wait a minute. I need to talk to you."

"Sure, Susan," he answered. "You know Francesca Mills, don't you?"

Judge Moreno nodded, and the two women exchanged strained smiles.

The strain was primarily Frankie's, however. She had just left Winnie Taylor, in whose company she had felt distinctly unattractive, and she was in no mood for the judge's dark beauty.

Judge Moreno looked at Frankie, and said to Blackie, "What I have to tell you is highly confidential."

Blackie shrugged. "I'll just tell her anyway," he said. "She might as well stay. And I'll tell you this, Susan. I have complete confidence in Frankie's discretion. She's a professional. She won't publish anything that doesn't need publishing."

Frankie stared at him with delight. He certainly made it difficult to stay mad.

"In that case," Judge Moreno said, "I just learned today that the Taylor inheritance was divided among the children."

"So?"

"Claudine Taylor told me personally that she intended to leave her estate to St. Andrew's Chapel, and she said that she had written a letter to that effect to Beaker Hogan. Father Robert Stickney was to be the executor."

"Beaker never mentioned it," said Blackie.

"As well he wouldn't," Judge Moreno replied scornfully, "since he intends to marry Winnie Taylor. . . . Maybe you're not aware of it, Blackie, but in probate cases, *intent* is extremely important. Just because Claudine died prematurely is no reason for the courts to disregard her last wishes."

"I see," said Blackie. "Well, it looks as if Beaker Hogan has a lot of explaining to do."

"He may just deny that he received such a letter," said Frankie.

"Claudine sent the letter," Judge Moreno said. "Proving it may be a different matter."

After the judge had gone, Frankie said, "Talk about motive. Beaker was afraid he'd lose out entirely if Claudine Taylor lived long enough to formally change her will."

Blackie said thoughtfully, "Something else, too. You're forgetting Winnie. She and Beaker were together the night Claudine was murdered. And her motive is every bit as strong as his. If he's involved, there's no reason to think she's not." He paused, and then said, smiling, "And now, how about that lunch you refused earlier? It's getting late and I'm starved."

She agreed and this time she took *his* arm.

"Don't treat me like a high school boy," he said derisively.

"You were never a high school boy," she answered with a grin.

13

I T was past four when Frankie and Blackie finished lunch. She regretted having accepted his invitation, for he had spent the entire hour passing thinly disguised romantic allusions.

She was not interested. She had agreed to lunch because of his qualified confidence in her, and because she was pleased that he still desired her company after being subjected to the dazzling good looks of Winnie Taylor and Susan Moreno. But her feelings had not changed. She had no wish to pursue anything other than a friendly, professional relationship. Why couldn't the stubborn bastard understand that? She had resolved to explain it to him—forcefully if necessary, when he astonished her by proclaiming, "I know all about your illness, Frankie. I called the clinic in Tyler."

"You what?" she exclaimed.

"It's amazing what you can find out when you're a cop."

"Now listen, you meddling fool! What right—"

"I care about you. And I don't care about your urostomy. I did some checking. Ostomates can live perfectly normal—"

Frankie gasped. "This is unbelievable! What possible indication have I given you to make you think that—" She stopped abruptly. She had established a fierce eye contact with him, but she could see that he was interpreting it as some sort of bond. She looked quickly away. "This is the most incredible invasion of privacy I've ever experienced. Don't you have any respect for me at all?"

"A great deal. That's why I wanted to find out what was wrong. I knew you were hurting. A simple kidney infection, you said. I didn't buy that at all."

She shook her head. "What else did they tell you?"

"Everything. That they're trying to determine if the cancer has returned—maybe the kidneys. But don't blame your doctor or his nurse. They had nothing to do with giving me the information. I've got other sources at the clinic. You know about sources."

She stood up and said softly, "As a newspaperwoman I use sources to preserve privacy and dignity. You've just shattered mine."

She walked slowly across the square with her head down, in the general direction of the *Kilkenny Weekly Times.* Blackie called to her several times from the doorway of the café, but she ignored him and continued on her way.

Her spirit was dark, and tears filled her eyes. One of the reasons she had left New York was so that she could keep her illness to herself. A new start in a new state. No more wondering whether or not her friends were pitying her or speculating morbidly on the nature of the appliance she wore under her clothes. Texas had offered a new beginning.

But Blackie Boone had snuffed it out with one telephone call. The arrogant son of a bitch. Who did he think he was? Now she would start to cringe again whenever people looked at her for more than a few seconds. Were they just being attentive, or were they wondering how she managed to pee through a hole in her side?

Maybe it wouldn't matter. Maybe the verdict on Friday would be more cancer . . . inoperable. That would make it simple. A few months and gone.

She knew she was feeling sorry for herself, but she didn't care. If *she* didn't feel sorry for herself, who would? Certainly not Dr. Ishikawa, the cold-blooded little quack. Him and his goddamn pediatric cancer. Sure those kids could be brave, they didn't have enough sense not to be.

She sniffed in satisfaction at her analysis, and then began

to laugh. Of course she understood exactly what she was doing, but self-pity can be so satisfying. And she felt she owed herself a little satisfaction.

She continued to chuckle as she rounded the corner of City Hall and headed for her office. But as she stepped off the sidewalk and into the street, a voice from behind her called, "Hey, Frankie, wait up!"

She turned to see a friend from *The Houston Post* scurrying across the grass and onto the sidewalk. She hurriedly wiped her eyes to remove any remaining tears, and said, smiling, "Can't you read?" She pointed to the sign that prohibited walking on the grass.

The reporter shrugged and said, "What's new in the Claudine Taylor murder case, Frankie?" If he noticed that her eyes were still red and moist, he didn't comment on it. He added, "I could sure use some help. The story's dying. I just can't go on saying they think someone from around here killed her. I need something fresh, different . . . or they'll call me back to Houston. How about the priest? Anything new there?"

"Why ask me?" she said.

"Everytime I see you you're with the chief of police. If anyone knows anything, you do."

She felt a momentary desire to forget the murders completely and to continue to wallow in self-pity; but the newspaperwoman in her began to surface, and she stopped to consider just what she did know: She was certain that both murders—and Karen Erikson's suicide as well—were related. She knew that Beaker Hogan and Winnie Taylor had a lot of questions to answer about Claudine Taylor's will. She knew that the killer or killers probably had the combination to Claudine's safe and the keys to her house. And she knew that this reduced the number of suspects to seven: Jake, Greg, and Winnie Taylor; James and Beta Lan Franco; and Edgar Brooks and Beaker Hogan. She knew that Father Stickney probably had visited Claudine Taylor on Saturday night, and she had a strong suspicion that there was something tangible involved, maybe something that Claudine had given to Father Stickney—something that the killer was looking for at Fairfield and St. Andrew's. She knew there were no meaningful fingerprints at Fairfield or St. Andrew's, no tire marks in the gully where the killer waited for Charlie Swicegood to pass, no unexpected evidence in the medical examiner's report. She knew that Claudine Taylor's torture was probably faked, and that Father Stickney's was probably real. She wondered what else she'd seen or heard that was important but which she was just not perceptive enough to understand.

She said to the reporter, "I really don't know anything that you don't. Chief Boone's just an acquaintance, and we haven't spent that much time together."

"Yeah, okay, Frankie," he answered cynically. "I appreciate the help. I'll return the favor one day."

And she was sure he would.

Her news instinct had now completely pushed aside her personal problems, and she turned back toward City Hall. Beaker Hogan and Winnie Taylor might still be inside, and there was no reason why she shouldn't question them herself—as a member of the press. If Hogan refused to cooperate that'd be all right, too. She'd just print Judge Moreno's remarks about Claudine Taylor's letter, and state that the mayor refused to comment on the matter. But if he hoped to succeed Jake Taylor in the House of Representatives, or even stay on as mayor, he'd have to open up sooner or later.

As she climbed purposefully up the City Hall steps, she felt a slight pain in the lower right quadrant of her back, but it quickly disappeared, and she put it down to the wide range of emotions she'd experienced in the past half hour.

"That's the most ridiculous thing I've ever heard," Beaker Hogan exclaimed. "Of course I didn't receive such a letter!"

"How do you explain Judge Moreno's statement?" asked Frankie.

Winnie Taylor said coldly, "We don't have to explain it at all, Mrs. Mills. It's up to Susan Moreno to explain, not us."

Mayor Hogan held up his hand. "No, that's not true, Win.

I'm in the public eye. And I hope to increase that exposure. Our rights are not the same as ordinary citizens'. . . . How do I explain Susan's statement? Simple enough. It's true. Susan Moreno is above reproach. If she says Claudine told her she'd sent me such a letter, then I'm sure the conversation took place. However, that doesn't mean that I *received* the letter. Claudine could've been speaking loosely. She might have been thinking of sending such a letter, and might have told Susan that she'd already done so. Naturally that doesn't prove intent in any degree, since nothing was placed in writing, and she might very well have changed her mind. That's something we'll never know, Mrs. Mills. . . . But there you have the answer you were looking for."

"Well, I have an answer," said Frankie. "And you're right. It was the one I was looking for. Remind me to look you up when I need a lawyer."

In the hallway outside Beaker Hogan's office, Frankie saw Blackie Boone approaching from the front entrance. He looked for a moment as if he were going to quicken his pace and call out for her to stop, but he seemed to sense the futility of it, and continued plodding toward her. She turned and walked rapidly out of the building in the opposite direction.

Winnie Taylor lowered herself onto Beaker Hogan's lap and kissed him lingeringly on the mouth. She stroked him gently and said, "Did Mother send you that letter?"

"What do *you* think?" he said, slipping his hand inside her blouse.

"I don't know."

"Do you really want to know?"

She responded to his caresses by burying her face in his neck. And then, breathing heavily, she raised her head and said, "No, I guess not. But one thing, Beaker."

"What's that?"

"I know you left the cabin Sunday night."

He inclined his head. "I thought you were asleep."

"I know."

"I went for a long walk. I had something on my mind."

"Like that letter?"

He smiled. "If there was a letter, I might have been concerned about it. I might have been thinking of ways to talk your mother out of leaving her money to the Church. I didn't drive to Fairfield and kill her, if that's what you're thinking. I couldn't kill anyone."

"I know that," she said, resting her head on his chest.

14

FALSE hope. Frankie sneered as she remembered how she had been encouraged by the fact that the severe pain had not recurred. Well, it was here now—searing, torturous, the worst ever—a fire in her lower back. She was bent over in her chair, which she had pushed back from her desk. Her arms were wound into a useless knot in her lap. She coughed and gulped for air. She released a low, animal-like groan, and coughed again.

Two men stood over her. Shock had immobilized them. They stared at each other dumbfounded, and neither appeared anxious to make the first move.

Bishop Benjamin Foster broke the trance first. "What's happened to her?" he said to Gabe Sullivan. "Is she ill?"

"Not that I know of," the old printer replied, his expression revealing worry and uncertainty.

The priest knelt beside Frankie's chair and thrust his face against her face. "How can we help?" he whispered. "Please tell us."

With her head down she mumbled, "My medicine . . . in my purse."

Gabe Sullivan reacted by darting into the press room. He returned, holding a glass of water, just as Bishop Foster triumphantly raised the bottle of Tylenol and codeine above Frankie's purse.

She looked up and said breathlessly, "The water first, Gabe, please."

When she had taken the medicine, she lowered her head once again and continued to moan softly.

After several minutes the pain began to diminish, and she said weakly, "Sorry. . . . I'll be all right."

Bishop Foster put his arm around her and said, "Of course you will. And we're right here with you."

Three or four more minutes passed with no one speaking. Frankie remained coiled in her chair and perfectly still. Finally she stirred and slowly raised her head. She patted Bishop Foster's hand, which firmly gripped her right shoulder. "Thanks, I may become a Catholic before this is all over."

The bishop smiled and said, "It seems that every time I see you, you're at a disadvantage. Did your fainting at St. Andrew's last night have anything to do with this?"

She shook her head. "No, that was plain, old-fashioned terror. This is something else." She hesitated. ". . . Kidney infection. Bothersome, and painful as all hell, but not serious."

He helped her to her feet, but she found that she was still unsteady, so she sat back down.

Gabe Sullivan said, "Shall I get the doctor, Mrs. Mills?"

"No, Gabe," she replied. "I'll be okay. I have a doctor's appointment in the morning. I'll be fine till then."

She coughed and looked slowly around the room to regain her composure and to make time to consider what had happened to her during the past quarter hour.

She had returned to her office after her interview with Beaker Hogan and Winnie Taylor, and had been pleasantly surprised to find Bishop Foster waiting for her. He had been highly excited, and had explained with a grin that he had been inspired by her comments on his abilities as a detective. He carried a small package under his arm.

Her excitement had risen to match his, because she sensed that he had discovered something important. But at that point she had been sidetracked by the onset of the pain, and had been unable to respond.

Now, the pain subsiding, she felt her curiosity returning, and she began to look for the package. She spotted it lying on the floor where the bishop had apparently tossed it when he knelt to help her. She motioned with the back of her hand. "What is it you've found, Bishop Foster?"

He turned toward the discarded package, but then turned back and replied, "Not now. *You* first. I'm worried about *you.*"

"No, no. Don't be," she assured him. "Everything's under control now. You've found something at the chapel, haven't you?"

He nodded reluctantly.

She prompted him by adding, "What is it? Please show me. I need to get my mind off myself."

He scooped up the package and placed it in front of her on the desk. "I think this is what the killer was searching for," he said. "And I think it tells us who he is."

Gabe Sullivan moved closer, and gave every indication that he was going to stay for the duration.

Frankie fingered the rumpled package, and asked, "How'd you find it?" She had wanted to blurt out, Who is he? But that would come. Now was the time to get all the answers— in the proper order.

Bishop Foster grinned. "Actually *you* put me on the right track. Remember you told me that the murders might be tied together? Well, I got to thinking about that and about the fact that the killer in both instances had been searching for something. And remember the note and the red chasuble and how we decided that Father Stickney probably went out to Fairfield Saturday night? Well, it was logical to conclude that Claudine Taylor called him out there so that she could give him something . . . which she did. Sunday night the killer tore up Fairfield looking for it, and then figured—correctly (and I can't tell you how)—that she'd given it to Stickney. The next morning . . . St. Andrew's." He spread his fingers and held his palms upward. "Same crime. Same scene. Same result. Nothing. He didn't find it."

"But you did?"

"You bet!" He pointed to his head. "Logic. First of all there must've been some reason for Claudine to want this"—he indicated the package—"out of the house. She must've felt threatened. When you read this you'll see why . . . and by whom. How he found out about it I don't know, but I'm sure that'll work itself out. Maybe you'll be able to fill in some of the missing pieces. . . . I should've taken this to the police first, I guess. But since you and I started in this together, I thought I'd come here first. We can take it to the police together."

"How'd you find it?" Frankie asked again.

"Oh, yes," he said. "Well, it was the rolling ladder."

She understood instantly. "Good Lord!" she said. "In one of the paintings."

He nodded. "There was no reason for the ladder to be there—in the middle of the wall. Those paintings hadn't been changed or rearranged since the last time I was at St. Andrew's."

"Which one was it?"

"What else? Bernadette of Lourdes. Stickney was a rather single-minded man. It was the first place I looked."

Gabe Sullivan appeared as if he were about to ask a question, but all that came out was an uncertain hum.

Frankie nervously fumbled with the string on the package. "May I?" she asked.

"That's why I brought it here."

She slowly peeled back the paper wrapping and deliberately pushed it aside. What remained was a discolored handwritten document, obviously many years old. She searched for a date and found one, faded and almost unreadable, buried in a deep wrinkle in the top right-hand corner: *Claudine Taylor, Fairfield. Kilkenny, Texas. September 8, 1958.* The narrative began about halfway down the page:

> *Curtis died today. I've never loved any other*
> *man, and I never will. He was my whole life. He*
> *was a good father and a wonderful husband. But*
> *he was an evil man. Cruel and violent (though*
> *never with me). He lived and died with one*
> *overwhelming preoccupation: money and the*

*power it generates. But maybe I can explain this
compulsion (though not excuse it), by
reminding whoever reads this that he grew up in
squalor on an Oklahoma tenant farm. This may
not be unusual in itself, many boys are thus
raised. What was unusual was that Curtis's
mother made their house a living hell with her
constant ranting over this condition. Curtis's
father finally could take no more and blew his
brains out with a shotgun. Curtis left that farm
with one thing in mind: get money, by any
means, as quickly as possible. As it turned out,
that means was murder.*

*The three of us—Curtis and I, and my brother
James, left Miami in 1940. We all knew there
was no future in Oklahoma. James's wife, Beta,
stayed behind because she had a job with the
telephone company, and it seemed impractical
to give it up.*

*We went to Dallas first, but couldn't seem to
get started there. We didn't know where to go
next or what to do. We were thinking of
returning to Oklahoma when a friend told us
about the East Texas oilfield and how the rumors
that it was too late to get in on it were false—
spread by producers who were anxious to add to
their holdings.*

*We came to Kilkenny in the summer of 1940,
and we found that indeed there were still
opportunities in the oilfield. But we had no
money and no one would give us credit. I went
to work as a beauty operator while James and
Curtis schemed about ways to put together a
stake.*

*I must point out that my brother was just as
desperately wicked as Curtis, though I can find
no rationale for his nature. He can be very
loving, but he is simply a bad man.*

In reading over what I have written so far, I seem to be painting a picture of myself as the innocent observer in all of this. That is not my intention. When I say that Curtis and James were evil, I hasten to add that I have been evil as well. I was aware of everything, and I am equally responsible. It is because of this guilt that I am driven to write this confession.

In the spring of 1941 we befriended the Eriksons. It was a calculated move. We knew that Samuel Erikson was very rich, and we coveted his money. Karen was one of my customers at the beauty shop, and we used that contact to establish the friendship. We had no definite plan in mind, but we were working on one, and we thought we knew the direction it would take.

Our greatest asset was my brother's good looks. He was a remarkably handsome man, strongly built, and very attractive to women. The fact that Karen was many years younger than Samuel had not escaped us, and we planned to exploit that difference.

James began his campaign slowly. He played the perfect gentleman—gracious, helpful, charming. But then he began to turn on the heat, and Karen fell like the little fool she was.

They continued their affair for six months— with James reporting back to us on every disgusting detail. I began to feel terribly guilty at this point, and wished we had never embarked on such a contemptible adventure. I had just discovered that I was pregnant with Jake, and that made me feel doubly guilty. I began to despise the way we were ridiculing Samuel and Karen's marriage. But I was totally dominated by Curtis and James, and I couldn't bring myself to object too strongly. And to be perfectly honest, I was as tired of being poor as they were.

I'm not sure what we were hoping for. Perhaps we thought that Karen might divorce Samuel, get a generous settlement, and then somehow give it to James. But we had a serious problem: James's wife, Beta. She was still back in Miami and was pressing to join us. Of course, Karen knew nothing of Beta, and had she found out, all of our schemes would've been knocked into a cocked hat.

Karen herself solved our problem for us. She had grown to hate Samuel, and late one afternoon, outside his office, she hit him over the head with a club. She continued to punish him until she thought he was dead.

She called James immediately and told him how much she loved him and what she'd done because of it. Curtis and James and I rushed to the scene, and while Karen waited inside the office, the three of us went out to inspect the body.

Samuel Erikson was not dead. In fact, by this time he was sitting up on the grass moaning. My husband and my brother didn't hesitate. After a quick, whispered conversation, they each picked up a piece of scrap lumber and, working in tandem, beat the old man to death. They swore me to silence, and we joined Karen. They told her that she had indeed killed her husband. James expressed shock and outrage that she could do such a thing. She cried and cried and protested that she'd done it so that they could be married. It was then that James told her he was already married, and that even if he were free, he would never marry a murderer.

At first I couldn't understand what they were

*up to. But when they agreed to help her cover up
the killing, and to make it look like robbery, it
all began to make sense. They intended to
blackmail her.*

*It was a good plan. They had her at their
mercy. They threatened to turn her in to the
authorities if she didn't sell off all of old
Samuel's assets and give the money to them. She
submitted easily. By now she had lost all heart,
and nothing mattered much to her anyway. By
the end of the year the transfer was complete,
and James and Curtis had their start.*

*They parlayed the windfall in the oilfield, and
the rest is common knowledge. We became
enormously wealthy. I can't say that it has been
wholly unpalatable. Frankly, it's been nice being
rich. But our foundation was built on sand, and
day by day I've grown more and more guilty.*

*And I'm beginning to discover the importance
of God in my life. I believe He is directing me to
write this confession. Curtis has gone on to his
eternal destiny, and I am left to tell this story.*

*James is still alive, of course. And I know that
making this public will destroy his life. That
can't be helped. We both will just have to accept
responsibility for our actions.*

*The children, too, will suffer. But in the long
run they will thank me for this. The family's
foundation must be rebuilt on the rock.*

Frankie looked up at Bishop Foster and Gabe Sullivan.
"Good God, she wrote this twenty-five years ago!"

"Is it true?" asked the old printer.

"Why wouldn't it be?" said Frankie. "It wouldn't be very
logical for her to make this stuff up."

"Looks like we've got our killer," Bishop Foster said. "It's
obvious what happened."

Frankie nodded. "She was finally going to make this public. She sure took her time, I'll say that. From the tone of the thing it looked like she was going to publish it in 1958. Wonder what happened."

The priest said thoughtfully, "Well, it's understandable. Her husband had just died. She was expiating. The very act of writing released a tremendous amount of pressure. But after a few days she began to think about it. Her brother was still alive; and then there were her kids, and herself for that matter. It got easier and easier to delay."

"But why now?" Gabe Sullivan asked.

"Bad heart, from what I've heard," Bishop Foster said. "And she was getting more and more religious. Father Stickney was a powerful influence. She probably dug this thing out of mothballs, and resolved that now was the time to take her punishment."

"Not to mention Karen Erikson," said Frankie. "She visited Claudine Saturday."

The bishop whistled softly. "I didn't know that. Uh-huh. That may have been the trigger."

Frankie got up and tested her legs. She stretched uncertainly and said, "You wondered how the killer found out about this confession. I think it's pretty clear."

"Let's call him by name," said Bishop Foster. "It's obvious that James Lan Franco's our man."

Frankie said, "Right. Well, here's the way I see it: Claudine runs into Karen and invites her to Fairfield. When she sees how ruined Karen is, the guilt swells to the breaking point. She confesses . . . tells Karen that she hadn't really killed Samuel, and that James and Curtis had just used her. Karen is horrified, of course, but is too tired and old by now to raise much of a fuss. Suicide has been on her mind for a long time. Claudine goes on to tell her that she has written a confession, and is now—at long last—going to make it public. Karen then goes to see James Lan Franco—we know she went to his house Saturday night—"

Bishop Foster interrupted. "Well, that settles it then. A child could divine the rest. Karen Erikson confronts Lan Franco with what she knows, and tells him about Claudine's intentions. . . . And then, seeing the futility of her life, returns to the Ramada Inn to kill herself."

Frankie picked up the thread. "And James Lan Franco calls Claudine in a fury to warn her not to release the confession. He threatens her and probably says something about coming out and taking it away from her. And maybe she brings up Father Stickney's name and inadvertently signs *his* death warrant."

The bishop nodded slowly. "It *had* to be like that. Lan Franco stews about it for a day, and then Sunday night goes out to Fairfield and kills her and tears up the place looking for the confession."

Frankie said, "And he tried to make it look like an intruder. . . . He stews some more, and then Monday morning"—she made a violent gesture—"Father Stickney!" She frowned. "Say, we think we've got this down pat, but what if our assumptions are all wrong?"

"I don't think they are," Bishop Foster said. "What do you think, Gabe?"

The printer shrugged. "Can't say. It makes sense. But I don't think James Lan Franco could murder his sister."

Frankie said, "By the way, Bishop, did you know that he's in the hospital . . . dying? Liver disease."

"Yes, I know. The courts may be relieved of the difficulty of convicting a rich man." He paused and gathered up the package on Frankie's desk. "Now it's time to go to the police with this. Come along. We'll get the credit together."

She shook her head. "No, Bishop Foster, you go. You've got it down as well as I do. And if I know Chief Boone, you won't have to do much explaining after he reads that. He's the real detective in this town."

15

BLACKIE Boone sat cheerlessly in his office at City Hall. He was attempting to concentrate on the results of his interview with Beaker Hogan and Winnie Taylor, but his thoughts kept returning to Francesca Mills. He realized now that he'd destroyed his relationship with her—if there had ever been a relationship. He should never have stuck his nose into her business by calling the clinic in Tyler; better yet, he should never have *told* her that he'd called. He was glad that he'd found out about her illness, but he should have kept it to himself. She would have told him when the time was right. Now his chances with her were nil.

The thought depressed him further. During the past year, he'd grown to admire everything about the spirited newcomer. He abhorred weak, superfluous Southern women with their polite masks and vicious souls. He'd already suffered through two appalling marriages with such women— both of whom could scarcely wait until the preacher said "Now you can" to make it clear that they'd rather not. Frankie was like a breath of fresh air. What you saw was what you got. She wasn't the prettiest thing in Gregg County, kind of tall and bony and loose-jointed; and she was almost fifty. But hell, he wasn't any prize catch either—what with his weight and all. And he certainly wasn't any youngster: fifty-one and looked every day of it.

He forced his mind to return to Beaker Hogan and Winnie

Taylor. He'd just completed an extended interview with them in Beaker's office (following on Frankie's heels apparently), and he was convinced that Beaker was lying about Claudine Taylor's will. But there wasn't a goddamned thing he could do about it, and he knew that the will would stand. Equal portions for Jake, Greg, and Winnie Taylor. The question was, did Beaker's chicanery have anything to do with Claudine Taylor's murder?

He looked up to see Bishop Benjamin Foster standing in the open doorway. The priest smiled, and with a minimum of explanation, laid the parcel containing Claudine Taylor's fading confession on the desk.

For the next ten minutes Blackie read the document with intermittent grunts while Bishop Foster sat quietly and smoked a cigar. When Blackie finished reading he continued to sit with his head down for several seconds. Finally he looked up, his eyes filled with cynicism and resignation.

"Interesting, eh?" said Bishop Foster.

Blackie nodded. "And you say you found it at St. Andrew's? I thought we were more thorough than that. . . . Yes, interesting." He paused and sighed. "Those miserable sons of bitches. . . . Rotten pair. Claudine, too—no matter how she tries to rationalize here." He motioned toward the sheets of paper scattered before him. "I wonder, is the whole family rotten?"

"It doesn't work that way, Chief Boone."

"No, I guess not." He considered the priest for a moment and then shrugged. "But to be honest with you, the kids are none too impressive either—including our prospective United States senator."

Bishop Foster smiled tolerantly. "There's rather a large gap between impressiveness and rottenness."

The two men continued to discuss the confession with occasional sharp philosophical asides. It was obvious that both were enjoying the conversation and were reluctant to bring it to an end. Finally the bishop began to point out some of the implications that he and Frankie had explored.

"Francesca Mills!" Blackie said, startled.

"Why, yes. I showed it to her before I came over here. We had sort of a comradeship in this thing because of the incident at St. Andrew's last night. I hope I haven't offended you, or done anything against the law."

"No, no," said Blackie quickly. "Claudine's confession *should* be published. And Frankie's the one to do it, as far as I'm concerned. As soon as we get the legalities out of the way, we'll see that she gets a copy. . . . No, I was just surprised, that's all. I respect her opinion. What did she have to say about it?"

The priest recounted his and Frankie's analysis at some length, concluding with, ". . . And then we decided that Justice may be raising her head in the guise of James Lan Fanco's cirrhosis of the liver."

Blackie tossed off a smile and said, "How is Frankie?"

"Not well, I'm afraid. When I first arrived she experienced a shocking episode of pain. Something's terribly wrong with her. She says it's a simple kidney infection. I hope that's all it is."

Blackie leaned forward. "I hope so, too," he said, frowning.

After Bishop Foster had gone, Blackie walked to the window and stared into the dark night. He thought about Frankie and what she had endured for the past several years. She was a remarkable woman. Her personal pain and suffering had surely been intense, and yet she had not turned inward. She was still deeply interested in the world around her and how she could alter it. He wondered if there was more bad news in store for her at the Tyler Diagnostic Clinic. He could find out easily enough. After her tests were completed, he could pick up the phone, and her file would be read to him—word for word. But he knew that he would never make such a call again. He had already violated her privacy, perhaps beyond the point of no return, and he had no desire to turn her disgust into hatred.

He thought about Claudine Taylor's confession. It was what had been missing all along—a hook for the case to hang on. Now the evidence could be reevaluated in relation to that hook. It certainly appeared that the document made James Lan Franco the prime suspect. His motive was the strongest, without question. Forty years ago he had murdered a helpless old man, and he had now killed again—twice—to cover up that ancient crime. It made perfect sense.

He returned to his desk and pulled out a three-by-five card from a small metal file. In the top left-hand corner printed in capital letters was the name JAMES LAN FRANCO. Beneath the name were several short headings, including *alibi, combination to safe,* and *keys to Fairfield.* Next came *motive,* followed by a large blank space. He rubbed his face, then wrote: *Fear of exposure. Sister's confession makes him a murderer. Stickney given confession for safekeeping.*

He replaced the card and locked the metal box in the top right-hand drawer of his desk. He then resumed his position at the window and continued to stare into the night.

At Fairfield, Edgar Brooks surveyed the room as Jake Taylor answered stale questions from a small group of reporters. Wednesday night, he thought, and already the story was running out of gas. In a few days it'd be dead and buried, and the media would be off on some new romp. And that suited him just fine.

He lumbered toward the table of hors d'oeuvres that he had instructed Jake to furnish for the press. As he reached for a stuffed mushroom he heard a bored reporter ask a disturbing question. He turned quickly to listen to Jake's reply.

"Yes," Jake said slowly, "my uncle is seriously ill. He was taken to the hospital this afternoon. It's been a week of tragedy. His prognosis is poor. He said that one of his greatest disappointments is that he may not be here to see me sworn in as a United States senator."

Edgar nodded approvingly.

"What's wrong with your uncle?" the reporter asked.

"Well . . . shock from his sister's . . . my mother's death has probably brought on"—he paused and looked at Ed-

gar—"a long-standing problem with the cellular structure of
his liver. The healthy cells—"

"Cirrhosis?" the reporter cut in contemptuously.

"Well, yes," said Jake. "But that's a term that covers a
great many—"

"Thank you," said the reporter.

There go the Baptists, Edgar thought helplessly. He
popped another mushroom into his mouth and walked
heavily toward the makeshift podium. His sinuses ached and
he wished he could go home to Longview. He wanted nothing more tonight than a hot bath and a good night's sleep.
He rubbed his face with both hands and wondered if he
would ever get a good night's sleep again.

"Has the President called again?" a reporter asked.

"No," Jake replied, "but the director of the FBI has con-
tacted us to offer the assistance of his agency. . . . He seems
to think there may be matters of national security involved
here."

"What matters? Did you keep government information in
your mother's safe?"

"Well, no but—"

"I'm the one who spoke to the director," Edgar interrupted. He didn't like the way the press conference was
going, and he had no intention of letting Jake make a bigger
fool of himself than he already had. "The director was calling—at the *suggestion* of the President. His approach was to
inquire whether or not we thought there were national security matters involved. And to assure us, if we did, that the
agency would back us all the way. There are also other reasons why the FBI gets involved in a case—state lines and
such—and the director stands ready to explore those areas
with us also. But as of now no one has seen any need to
bring in federal authorities."

"What about the local police?"

"They're doing the best they can," Edgar answered.

"What about the theory that someone from around here
committed these murders?"

Jake said patronizingly, "That seems to be Chief Boone's idea. He has a hodgepodge of reasons for that theory. You'll have to ask him."

Edgar attempted to change the subject. "Gentlemen, let's not forget that there are national and international issues to ask about. Maybe they're not as sensational, but the country at large is still concerned with such things as unemployment and foreign policy."

The reporters remained stubbornly silent, so he tried to prompt them by quoting from one of Jake's position papers on the Middle East. When no one responded, he took Jake's arm and led him away from the podium.

But before the reporters could rise, Beaker Hogan and Winnie Taylor came into the room.

Edgar groaned inwardly. He didn't like Beaker Hogan or Jake's sister. Winnie was distant and dangerously unpredictable and Beaker was provincial and self-serving. Their presence made him extremely uncomfortable. He had agreed to Beaker's congressional candidacy only because Jake had insisted, and because the additional publicity might help Jake's Senate race. Nevertheless, he affected a big smile and said, "Winnie, Beaker, come on in. Maybe the press would like a few shots at Jake's successor in the House of Representatives."

A wire service reporter asked quickly, "Mayor Hogan, Judge Susan Moreno says that Claudine Taylor intended to leave her money to the Catholic Church, and that you—as the family lawyer—were sent a letter to that effect. How do you answer her?"

"With great care," Beaker replied confidently, striding to Jake's vacated podium. "Susan Moreno's my friend, and I have the greatest respect for her. I know she believes I received such a letter. But I assure you I didn't. As far as I know, Claudine's wishes hadn't changed. Her will is clear and above contest. I'm sorry Susan's felt it necessary to go public with her opinions. I'm sure upon reflection she'll regret her comments."

"Don't you feel a conflict of interest," the same reporter continued, "since you're marrying Winnie Taylor?"

"None at all. I've been in close contact with the family for many years. What has occurred between Winnie and me is only natural. I have no apologies to make."

Winnie broke in, "Mother was always making threats about her will. I'm afraid poor Judge Moreno was just listening to another of Mother's tirades. . . . Something along the lines of, 'If my children don't straighten up, Susan, I'll have to disinherit them.' God knows we heard the same thing often enough. Mother was a dear and we loved her, but she used her will like a hammer. I think Susan Moreno needs to take a course on listening. I understand several are available."

Edgar Brooks watched Winnie Taylor's cold, satisfied smile, and renewed his intention to stay as far away from her as possible.

He walked to the podium and turned to face the press. "That's it for now," he said sternly. "It's clear that you're hung up on these terrible events—understandable, of course." He smiled tolerantly. "But next time let's remember that we have two candidates for national office, okay? It's a big country and a big world."

In his suite at Curtis Taylor Memorial Hospital, James Lan Franco, his face turned to the wall, listened dully while the assembled doctors discussed his case among themselves as if he were not present. The specialist from Dallas droned on about the medical intricacies of cirrhosis of the liver and about exactly what kind of damage alcohol does to the susceptible organ. Dr. Presley and the others grunted appropriately during the great man's pauses, and occasionally interrupted with questions obviously designed to demonstrate that they were pretty smart fellows themselves. James wanted to puke, but he didn't have the energy. He had just been told that he had no future and that he would probably never leave the hospital. Couldn't these fools understand how meaningless their conversation was to a man who had just heard his death sentence pronounced?

He turned his head to look at Beta. She sat curled up in a straight-back chair, her chin on her knees, her face red and swollen from crying. She caught his eye and shook her head slowly and helplessly. He turned back to face the wall.

For a brief moment he thought about God. Was there any hope at all for a man who had lived as he had lived? He supposed not. He supposed that if there were an afterlife, he would be in for it all right. He'd be a fool to think that heaven was reserved for murderers.

Greg Taylor was almost six feet tall and thickly built, but he felt small and vulnerable as he sat across from the massive young man in the red jogging outfit.

"What's on your mind, Greg?" the young man asked.

"I drove over tonight to assure you that there'll be plenty of money for the trip to Washington—and for anything else the committee needs in the future."

The young man smiled his approval and said, "That's good, that's real good!" His smile widened into a bright grin that pleased Greg and made him glad he had made the special trip to Tyler. "You've got your priorities right," the young man added. "We've got to stop this nuclear insanity. The freeze movement's our last hope."

"I knew you'd want to know, Arnie," said Greg, his face reddening.

"It makes it easier for sure. Now we'll take everyone. We'll shout down Congress if we have to. No more wars. No more bombs. No more old men sending us to do their dying for them." He grinned again, but this time held back a little as if he understood the effect he was having on Greg.

"Tell the others for me, will you, Arnie? Tell them there'll be no problem with money in the future."

"They already know."

"But how—"

"They knew you'd do the right thing."

Greg nodded feebly. ". . . Well, tell them I'm glad they feel that way. I feel the same way about all of you." He held the big man's gaze for several seconds and then added, "I've never felt closer to anyone. You're my real family."

16

WHEN Frankie arrived at her office on Thursday morning, Blackie Boone was waiting for her.

"What do you want?" she said coldly.

"I came to apologize."

"An apology's no good. You went too far."

"I know."

"You presumed far too much."

"I know."

"I'm not interested—"

"I know that, too. How're you feeling? Bishop Foster said you had a bad time last night."

For a moment Frankie felt her anger rise, but she shrugged and said, "Pretty good. Last night was bad, but it seems to have passed. I go back to the doctor this morning for the last of my tests. But you already know that, don't you?"

He said, "I won't violate your privacy again."

At that point Gabe Sullivan came in, and Frankie spent several minutes instructing him regarding some advance layouts for next Monday's edition. She then turned back to Blackie.

"What did you think of Claudine Taylor's testament?"

"I suppose I should be shocked," he replied, "but I'm not. Nothing shocks me anymore."

"What does James Lan Franco say about it?"

"Haven't been back to the hospital yet. . . . Later today. Want to be there?"

"Yes."

"I'm going to Tyler first," he said, "then to Longview. James looks guilty as hell, but there're still three alibis to check—Greg's, Jake's, and Edgar's. The case looks wrapped up, but I want to get all the facts together . . . put the final stitches in this thing. Want to ride with me? I could wait for you at the clinic, and then we could do some interviews together. We were getting to be a pretty good team until I screwed it up."

She hesitated.

"Strictly professional," he added quickly, "and just friends."

"In that case, yes," she said. "I'd like to see where some of these threads end."

Frankie knew that neither Dr. Ishikawa nor his nurse was responsible for giving her medical information to Blackie Boone, but nevertheless she felt a sense of betrayal as she waited in the examination room for them to appear. She wondered if she should tell Dr. Ishikawa about the unprofessional, and probably illegal, behavior of someone at the clinic, but as she thought about it she decided that such an accusation would serve no purpose. The real issue now was the state of her health.

The door opened and Dr. Ishikawa's nurse entered the room.

"Hello, Norma," Frankie said.

"Frankie, hello again." The matronly nurse walked to the long sink and officiously rearranged several small bottles that were scattered on the counter. Busywork, Frankie thought. Did Norma know something? Something dreadful? Was she acting busy to keep from giving anything away?

Dr. Ishikawa came in next. His head was down and he was reading from a clipboard.

"Good morning, Mrs. Mills. It's been a long week. Are you holding up okay?"

"Yes, Doctor, thank you. Do you have anything to tell me yet?"

"We need today's tests. Everything's got to be checked and cross-checked."

"Surely you have some idea."

"There are indications."

"Like what? Do I have more cancer? Are my kidneys involved?"

"You're asking me to make an evaluation without all the facts."

"Damn right! In fact I insist on it."

"We could be wrong. Today's tests will give us a definitive answer."

"What's wrong with me?"

The young doctor laid the clipboard on the counter and shook his head. "You're a very difficult patient, Mrs. Mills. You must appreciate medical procedure."

"The hell with medical procedure! What do you think so far?"

"We think you have a kidney tumor."

Frankie lowered her head and didn't respond for several seconds. Finally she said, "Are you certain?"

"No. You insisted . . . remember?"

She nodded. "Malignant?"

He shrugged his shoulders.

"Are kidney tumors often malignant?"

"You're racing ahead, Mrs. Mills. These questions are hypothetical."

She ignored him. "Is kidney cancer common?"

"Not very. Nine or ten thousand deaths a year."

"What can be done?"

"A number of things. Interferon therapy has been used at M.D. Anderson Hospital. There's been some success. A halt or slowdown in the spread of tumors . . . reduction in size—"

"Should I go to Houston?"

"Mrs. Mills, we're not even sure you *have* a tumor. And if you do, we don't know what type."

"I've been through all this before," she said too loudly. "I know I've got one, and I *know* it's malignant. I went through all that false-hope bullshit two years ago. I'm not playing that game again."

An hour later she stumbled weakly toward Blackie Boone's waiting patrol car. She felt sick to her stomach and terribly depressed. She wished she had never agreed to ride with him. She wished she were alone. She desired nothing more than to creep back to Kilkenny and hide in her bed until tomorrow.

But when she saw Blackie's large head slumped against the headrest, she gulped a deep breath of air and forced a smile.

"Hey, wake up!" she called, pounding on the door. "We've got work to do."

He opened his eyes and scooted up in the seat. "Frankie. Whew! Sound asleep. Tireder than I thought." He leaned over and opened the passenger door. When she was inside, he asked, "You all right?"

"Fine. I feel like an old suitcase that's been through baggage pickup one too many times . . . but I'm okay."

He looked her over carefully and appeared as if he were about to ask another question, but instead ground his key in the ignition. The supercharged engine began to whine.

"Let's go see the no-nukes crowd," he said.

The headquarters for the East Texas Nuclear Freeze Committee was a half-century-old, wood-frame, two-story house in one of Tyler's least attractive neighborhoods. Some effort had been made to renovate the structure. The front facade had been splashed with red paint, and several small brick planters had been erected to give the appearance of cleanliness and order. But the sides of the building, which were clearly visible from the street, had not been touched; the dirty white walls were flaked and peeling, and the shutters were rotted and cockeyed.

A sign dangling from the roof of the porch proudly declared the committee's presence; but as Frankie glanced around she could see that such an identification was unnecessary. The bumper stickers on the cars parked up and down the street were testimony enough. No Nukes; one nuclear bomb can spoil your whole day; Freeze Now; and even Question Authority.

"Five men and two women," said Blackie under his breath as he pulled to a halt.

"I beg your pardon," Frankie said.

"Thinking out loud. . . . Five men and two women had the combination to that safe. The Taylor kids, the Lan Francos, and Hogan and Brooks. It *had* to be one of them, though I don't think either of the women could've managed the actual killings. . . . It's probably James—that's logical."

"What about a hired killer?"

"Possible. But we can't think about that. What we don't need is more complication. We need to simplify. If it turns out to be a hired killer, so be it."

"Let's talk about motives," said Frankie. She was still depressed, and it was still an effort to sustain her concentration, but she felt a slight charge of adrenaline as they discussed the murders. Cancer or not, she was still a newspaperwoman.

"The confession and the inheritance," Blackie said slowly. "It's there somewhere—one of the two. Maybe both. One of those seven killed Claudine and the priest to make sure that the confession didn't get out . . . or to keep the money in the family."

Frankie said, "If it's the money, I'd bet on Beaker Hogan and Winnie Taylor."

"Greg Taylor needs money, too," said Blackie. "Jake's got all he needs—if the rich ever get enough. I wonder if Jake and Greg knew about Claudine's plan to disinherit them." He put his hand on the door handle and began to push downward.

Frankie stopped him. "I think it's the confession," she said. "I'm not sure why. I think because of Father Stickney's murder. His death was pointless if it's just the will. With Claudine gone, he could jump up and down for a week and still not get a cent. . . . It had to be the confession."

"Then who benefits? Who gains the most from its suppression?"

"James Lan Franco, of course."

Blackie nodded. "I don't see Winnie or Beaker getting too concerned about the confession. Why should they care? Smirch up the family name a bit, but that's not their kind of thing."

"Or Greg's," said Frankie. She waved her arm toward the old house. "Preserving the Taylor name wouldn't interest him either." She put her hand to her mouth and said thoughtfully, "But Jake Taylor would have a critical stake in keeping Claudine's confession secret. He'd never get elected to the Senate if it got out. He'd be hounded out of politics . . . will be, because this is all coming out, you know. And Edgar Brooks—that slimey little man would understand all of this."

Blackie smiled. "We're forgetting something else: Beaker's running for office, too. That puts Winnie and him back into the confession derby. Damn. I'm trying to simplify all this and it just gets more complicated."

"Thank God for James Lan Franco," said Frankie. "He'll probably admit it all and we'll be home free."

"Let's hope so."

They were met at the door of the old house by a neatly dressed young woman with close-cropped blond hair and a round pixie face. Good God, thought Frankie, a college cheerleader. Whatever happened to the scraggly protesters of the sixties, with their ratty hair and wire-rimmed glasses?

The young woman greeted them warmly and asked them to come in. Though she must have been curious about Blackie's uniform, she didn't inquire about their business until she had made them quite comfortable in the old-style drawing room.

"We're here to talk about Greg Taylor," said Blackie pleasantly. "My name is Garner Boone. I'm the chief of police in Kilkenny. And this is Francesca Mills." Frankie smiled as she realized that he had intentionally left the impression that they were both with the police.

"What about Greg?" the young woman asked.

Before Blackie could answer a tall, athletic man, about twenty-five or twenty-six, bounded down the stairs and loped energetically into the room.

"Hello there," he called out cheerfully. "What's up here?"

"Arnie," the young woman said, "these people are with the Kilkenny Police. This is Chief Boone and this is Francesca Mills. They've come to talk to us about Greg Taylor. Maybe you'd better take over." She turned to Blackie and Frankie. "This is the chairman of our group, Arnie Kinard."

Blackie rose to shake hands and Frankie nodded politely.

Arnie motioned Blackie back to his seat and then took a seat himself. "This must be about Greg's mother's murder . . . right?"

"Right," said Blackie. "Routine stuff. We're just trying to verify everyone's whereabouts on Sunday night."

"Which is where we come in?"

"Right again. Greg says he was here—at a nuclear freeze meeting—most of the evening. Is that true?"

"Sure is. There were twenty, maybe thirty of us here that night. Pretty good alibi, if you ask me."

Blackie smiled. "Sure sounds like it. What time did the meeting start?"

"Around seven."

Frankie cut in, "And what time did the meeting break up?"

"Oh . . . around ten-thirty or so. But Greg hung around for a while. He didn't leave till eleven, maybe eleven-thirty."

"How many people hung around with him?" asked Frankie.

Arnie grinned and said, "Nearly everyone. No one goes straight home after our meetings."

"Almost an hour's drive to Kilkenny," Blackie mused aloud.

"At least that," said Arnie, grinning again. "Maybe *over* an hour if you're not a policeman and have to drive fifty-five."

They arrived in Longview just before noon, and headed for Will Stone's Sportsman's Paradise.

"Hungry?" Blackie asked.

"Not really," said Frankie, her head turned toward the window, "but I should eat something."

"Let's see if Will Stone's is open for lunch. Kill two birds with one stone." He chuckled at the wordplay, but Frankie continued to stare out the window.

The Sportsman's Paradise was tucked away in a small stand of pines, about a quarter of a mile off the highway. There were ten or twelve cars parked in the lot, and Blackie grunted that unless the place was greatly overstaffed they were probably serving lunch.

The menu was fashioned in the shape of a duck, and was filled with exotic offerings ranging from roast deer to grilled trout.

"Where the hell's the hamburgers?" asked Frankie. "The last thing I want for lunch is deviled muskrat."

Blackie laughed. "Me, too. Don't worry, every place's got hamburgers."

"Can you believe this menu?" said Frankie. "Look here— they've even got rattlesnake . . . fried. Is that the way they cook it here? In New York we always broiled our rattlesnakes."

Blackie laughed again. "Broiled's better, I'm sure. But look here, some of these things sound pretty good. Everyday's got its own special. Today's—Thursday's—is roast wild duck. I'll bet that's damned good. Wednesday's was buffalo—sounds tough. On Fridays they got brook trout—fresh. Saturdays it's deer, Sundays wild goose. Quite a place. But look at these prices. Not many cops eat here, I'll tell you that."

The waitress approached and Blackie said, "We need a couple of hamburgers, and we need to see Will Stone. Tell him it's Chief Boone and Francesca Mills from Kilkenny."

Will Stone came to the table just as they were finishing their hamburgers. He was a corpulent man who looked as if he had been sampling his own food for many years. He thrust out his hand to Frankie.

"Mrs. Mills, I'm Will Stone, how do you do? So you're the

one who bought the *Kilkenny Times,* eh? . . . Chief Boone, nice to see you again. You probably don't remember, but we've met before—several years ago, in Tyler."

Blackie nodded, but it was obvious that he didn't remember.

Frankie watched the restaurateur as he continued to talk effusively, and then thought, this man has been on the telephone . . . probably to Jake Taylor or Edgar Brooks. Why would he do that?

"Well, what can I do for y'all?" Stone said as he drew up a chair.

"No big deal," said Blackie. "Just doing some checking." He gestured toward Frankie. "I gave Mrs. Mills a ride to her doctor's. We'll be heading back to Kilkenny before long."

"How can I help?" Stone said nervously.

"Sunday night," Blackie replied. "Edgar Brooks and Jake Taylor—did they have dinner with you?"

"The night of that terrible murder? Yeah, they sure did. Did you get that guy yet? Killing an old woman. Some drifter from Louisiana, eh—something like that?"

"Still working on it. They did have dinner with you that night, then?"

"Sure did."

Frankie picked up the menu. "I love your place, Mr. Stone," she said. "I'm crazy about wild game. I almost ordered some today."

"You should have."

"Next time. We decided it was a bit much for lunch. My favorite's wild goose—I had it once, up in the Catskills. I never forgot it."

Blackie stared at her and smiled crookedly.

"Wild goose's our Sunday special," Stone said proudly. "It's delicious."

"Is that what Jake and Edgar had Sunday night," she said casually, ". . . wild goose?"

"Yeah, right. I sat down with them. Had some myself. Jake sent his compliments to the chef—the best cook in East Texas."

"You're a liar, Mr. Stone."

"What?" the fat man sputtered. "What did you say?"

"I said that you're a liar. Edgar Brooks and Jake Taylor weren't here Sunday night. They didn't have dinner with you."

Stone began to rise and to slide his chair backward at the same time. "You can't talk to me that way! Who do you think . . . Chief Boone, what's this woman . . . who does she think she is?"

Blackie sat with his chin resting in his hands. His eyes were calm and amused. "You'd better sit back down, Mr. Stone," he said sharply. "You may have dug yourself a hole that you can't crawl out of."

Stone resumed his seat and muttered, "You'd better be careful, Mrs. Mills."

Frankie snorted and took the offensive. She turned to Blackie. "Do you remember in your office, when Edgar Brooks told us that he and Jake had dinner at Will Stone's Sunday night? 'Great fish,' he said . . . not great wild goose, 'great fish.'" She turned back to Stone. "Do you think a couple of sophisticated gents like Jake and Edgar could mistake goose for fish? Not likely, I'd say. And you sat down and joined them, eh, Stone? And Jake sent his compliments to the chef? Did I make myself clear a moment ago? Maybe I didn't. Here, let me say it again. You're a liar, Mr. Stone . . . aren't you?"

The restaurateur lowered his eyes and did not look up. He mumbled something, but it was unintelligible.

"What was that?" asked Blackie. "What did you say?"

Stone looked up. "I said that some burglar killed that old lady, we all know that."

"We know nothing of the sort. Now, have you been lying or not? And let me warn you, you'd better tell the truth this time or I'll jump down your throat with both feet."

Stone lowered his head again. "Yeah, I guess I have been," he said softly but clearly. "They weren't here. Jake's got women—a lot of them. I guess he was with one of them."

* * *

It didn't take much to uncover the truth at the country club. When those savvy individuals learned that Will Stone had broken down, they cut Jake Taylor loose fast. No indeed, the two politicians had certainly *not* been at the country club Sunday night . . . and no one had ever said such a thing. *Of course* they would sign a statement to that effect. They would cooperate with the law in every respect—as they always did.

Barney's Nightclub—where Jake and Edgar had ostensibly stopped for drinks before moving on to the country club— proved a little more difficult, but not much. The owner and patrons had already discussed Sunday's events with Edgar Brooks, and they thought that maybe the two men had really been there that night. But after some judicious questioning by Blackie and Frankie, their assurance disappeared and they began to realize that no one actually remembered seeing the politicians. Perhaps they hadn't been there after all.

"Well, what've we really accomplished?" said Blackie, as they drove back to Kilkenny. "Muddied up the waters a bit . . . not much more. Greg's alibi looks flawless. Jake's and Edgar's—shot to hell. But that doesn't mean that either one of them had anything to do with the killings."

"We've still got James Lan Franco," Frankie said, staring out the window at the pine forest that lined both sides of the road. "He's got a lot of explaining to do. He might just lay it all out for us. He hasn't got much to lose, has he?"

Blackie shook his head. "No, he hasn't. . . . But if you think that dying men always tell the truth, you're wrong. I've seen men lie as they're roasting in the electric chair . . . right up to their last breath. It doesn't figure, but that's the way people are."

17

FRANKIE stood at the window in James Lan Franco's hospital room looking out across the parking lot toward the Kilkenny town square. She watched the shoppers darting in and out of the stores, the businessmen chatting on the street corner, and the old-timers strolling in the early summer sun. Life goes on, she thought. In the final analysis, each individual is totally separate from all others. Change is shrugged off and life goes on.

The room was quiet, except for the rustle of pages, punctuated by an occasional chuckle coming from James Lan Franco's hospital bed.

Blackie Boone, his hands resting authoritatively on his hips, stood next to Beta Lan Franco on the right side of the bed.

Officer Charlie Swicegood guarded the door as if the suspect, bedclothes and all, were about to burst through the door and flee to Mexico.

Frankie turned from the window just as the dying man finished reading Claudine Taylor's confession.

"So my little sister really did it," he said, tossing the document casually on the floor. He chuckled again, and put his hands behind his head.

"You don't seem too concerned," said Blackie, striding forward to retrieve the confession.

"Why should I be? It's a goddamn pack of lies. You've got to understand what kind of a woman Claudine was: hysterical, fanatic. More so the older she got. Hell . . . she dreamed up all this stuff in one of her religious fogs!"

"There are some pretty serious accusations," said Blackie. "Old man Erikson—"

"What is it, James?" Beta Lan Franco interrupted. "What was in those papers you were reading?" Her face was drawn from lack of sleep and her words were imprecise.

"It's nothing," James replied. "Claudine's dredged up some sludge from before the war. Pure crud. Blames Curtis and me for Samuel Erikson's death. If I remember right, the old fool was killed by a thief. . . . Claudine was crazier than that priest. She must've needed something to impress him in the confessional."

Blackie said, "So you deny that you murdered Samuel Erikson?"

"Goddamn right I do!"

Beta sat down weakly on one of the wooden chairs near the foot of the bed. She sighed and stared at the floor.

"You know this is nothing new," James added. "Claudine's been threatening this kind of nonsense for years. And I mean *years!*"

Frankie, who had taken the chair next to Beta, looked up in surprise. She wanted to ask a question, but decided against it.

Blackie said, "Your sister talked about doing this before?"

"She sure did."

"What was your response?"

"Same as it was this time. I told her I'd cram the goddamn thing—"

"This time?" said Blackie quickly.

James laughed. "Right, this time. I called her Saturday night—but you've already figured that out, haven't you?"

Blackie nodded.

"Well, sure I called her. I loved that crazy broad, but she could be a pain in the ass. Even though that confession is completely false, I didn't want it getting out. People believe what they want to believe."

"How did you find out about her intentions this time?" said Blackie.

"I think you already know the answer to that, but I'll tell you anyway. Karen Erikson told me. Claudine fed her this fantasy, and she ate it up. As you know, Karen came by our place Saturday night. She got half-crazy, and I kicked her out the French doors."

"Who else knew about Claudine's previous threats to tell this story?"

"Jake, me . . . Greg and Winnie, too. Jake and I talked about it any number of times."

Frankie rose and walked toward the bed. "Forgive me, Mr. Lan Franco," she said, "but would you mind if I asked you a question?"

"Go ahead. The newspapers are going to go wild with this anyway. Maybe you'll give my side."

"Did you call anyone else Saturday night besides Claudine?"

"Sure—Jake. I called him in Longview."

"What was his reaction?"

"Concern, of course. This nonsense could spoil his Senate chances."

"Anyone else?"

"No—just Jake and Claudine."

Blackie asked, "What did you do Sunday?"

"Started drinking. All this was getting me down. Stayed sloshed most of the day."

"And Sunday night?"

"Still drunk. I didn't stumble out to Fairfield and murder my sister if that's your point."

"But you threatened her on the telephone."

"Damn right. She needed threatening."

"Where were you Monday morning?"

"Home, asleep. Didn't get there until the sun was up. Charlie here took me . . . straight from your office. Beta was still asleep. I hadn't got her up when Charlie came earlier. I crawled into bed and slept till noon. Then I went out to Fairfield for a while."

Blackie looked toward Charlie Swicegood and Beta Lan Franco, both of whom nodded.

"You can believe me on all of this, you know," James said with a shrug. "I'll be dead before long. A man in my position doesn't lie."

Blackie looked at Frankie and smiled cynically.

The human mind often makes things more complicated than they are. It rejects the simple and the straight and searches for the difficult and the bizarre.

Frankie considered this principle as she walked across the hospital lobby toward the exit. For some time now she had been thinking about an approach to the murders that seemed ridiculously simple. But she had not pursued it because it had seemed too obvious, and also because James Lan Franco might have made it unnecessary by confessing.

She turned to Blackie, who was walking beside her. "What kind of knife was used on Claudine Taylor?"

"Standard hunting knife. Slightly curved blade. Must be ten thousand of them in this part of the country. Why?"

"I was thinking about the murder weapons."

Charlie Swicegood, who was on Frankie's other side, said, "The shotgun and the knife? We don't have the shotgun."

"I know, but I'm wondering if we've given them enough attention. Maybe we've neglected the most obvious evidence."

Blackie replied, "I've had the knife subjected to every conceivable test—believe me. I know more about it than I know about my family."

"Scientific attention," said Frankie. "That's not what I mean."

Charlie asked, "What do you mean, then?"

"They're common weapons, right?"

Both men nodded.

"Used in hunting?"

"Naturally," said Blackie patiently.

"Well . . . which of our suspects are hunters?"

"What difference would that make?" Charlie cut in. "He wouldn't have to be a hunter. He could've bought the gun and knife . . . in Dallas or someplace."

"Not on Sunday," said Frankie. "Not in Texas. And I don't think these murders were planned . . . at least not long-range. I think Saturday night was the key."

Blackie nodded. "You've got a good point. Where would the killer get a shotgun and a hunting knife between Saturday night and Sunday night? It bears checking into."

"Do you want me to pull the hunting licenses, Chief?" said Charlie, motioning toward City Hall. "Bring them to your office?"

"Yeah, would you, Charlie? I'd appreciate it."

"Why don't you wait with me?" Blackie said to Frankie. "We'll have the answer to your question in a few minutes."

A half hour later Officer Swicegood, a wry smile on his face, laid a gray copy of an official-looking form on Blackie's desk. The name at the top was clear.

"James Lan Franco likes to shoot birds," he said.

"Then we have—" Frankie began.

"However," Charlie added, "so do Beaker Hogan, Edgar Brooks, Jake Taylor, Winnie Taylor, and Beta Lan Franco. . . . They've all got licenses." He laid five more copies on the desk. "Apparently, the only one of this bunch who doesn't hunt is Greg Taylor."

"No, he wouldn't," said Frankie. "Well, it was just an idea." So much for simplicity, she thought. Back to the bizarre.

Officer Bobby Ridgeway crept reluctantly through the door to Blackie's office and said, "Chief, that priest's here to see you again."

"Send him in, Bobby."

Swicegood followed Ridgeway out the door, and soon Bishop Foster entered the room.

"Hello, Mrs. Mills," he said. "Chief Boone. How are you?"

"What's on your mind, Bishop Foster?" asked Blackie.

"Two things. I've had a talk with Judge Moreno. She tells me that someone may be needed to defend the Church's interests in the matter of Claudine Taylor's will. Second, I'm curious about what's happened with that old confession? After all, I'm the one who found it." He grinned proudly.

Frankie said, "James Lan Franco denied the whole thing, of course. Claimed his sister was hallucinating."

"Ah, a good answer," Bishop Foster replied appreciatively. "Hysterics are a way of life with these charismatics. Who can tell what the truth is?"

"Lan Franco's lying through his teeth," Frankie said angrily. "He killed that old man all right."

"Naturally," the bishop agreed, "but proving it is a difficult matter. I'm sure he killed his sister and Father Stickney, too. Any new evidence?"

Blackie shook his head. "No. And as far as the will goes, I don't know what to tell you. I know Susan Moreno believes that Claudine intended to leave everything to the Church— I believe it, too. But it's a little late. Not much we can do now."

Bishop Foster shrugged. "To tell the truth, I figured that. But I thought I'd poke my nose in anyway. The Church can always use the money." He sighed and tapped his cheek with his forefinger. ". . . So James Lan Franco's going to take his secrets to the grave. I rather thought he might come clean. Set the record straight. Prepare to meet his Maker."

"Maybe he expects a miracle," said Frankie. "Healing—a new liver."

"He'd need Father Stickney for that," Bishop Foster said, smiling, "and he killed him."

"We're on our way to Fairfield," said Blackie. "Want to come along? You can look out for the Church's interests, and frankly we can use another head in these murders."

"I'd love to," said the bishop excitedly. "Move over, Father Brown."

18

THE bishop's dark Cadillac sped smoothly down the highway toward Fairfield. The sweet smell of resin from the pine trees filled the car. Neither Frankie nor the priest spoke. It was that rare moment in the day, that special moment that is best enjoyed privately—the onset of twilight.

Frankie was glad she had insisted on taking two cars, and glad that she had consigned Blackie and Officer Swicegood to the patrol car. She was in no mood to have this spirit of restfulness destroyed by Blackie's irritating chatter, and besides, it was a perfect opportunity to remind him that he was not forgiven for his intrusion into her private life.

She slipped her hand to her side and felt for her appliance. It seemed all right. She had emptied it and carefully cleaned her stoma in the restroom at City Hall. She had wanted no unpleasant surprises at Fairfield. She cast a quick glance at Bishop Foster, but he was still staring straight ahead. A fine gentleman, she thought—graceful, poised, humorous. A candidate for lifetime friendship.

Lifetime, she mused. What exactly did that mean in her case? A few months? A year or two? Even now she could feel a dull ache in her kidneys, and a sharp prickly pain around her stoma. She wondered what nasty little tests Dr. Ishikawa was evaluating at this very moment.

And yet, remarkably, on the night before her sentencing, here she was racing out to Fairfield to continue her coverage of the murders. It reminded her of the story she'd read about the man on death row in Huntsville who was studying Latin. Impractical perhaps, but distinctly human.

The Cadillac left the highway and headed down the side road. Once they had cleared the stand of pines, the sunlight streamed in the windows, and Frankie was shocked to see how much of the day still remained. The countryside between the highway and Fairfield was open fields, and the sun's red ball leapt back over the horizon.

The earlier spell was broken. Bishop Foster spoke first. "About twenty minutes more, if I remember right. I don't see Chief Boone's car anywhere."

"They took off like bank robbers," said Frankie. "They're probably there by now."

When the priest brought the heavy sedan to a sudden stop on Fairfield's gravel driveway, Frankie said, "You see, there they are," pointing toward Blackie and Charlie, who stood beside the patrol car, talking to a small knot of reporters.

Frankie's friend from *The Houston Post* recognized her while she was still in the car, and walked sullenly to her window. He leaned in and said, "We can't get anything from the cops. Are you going to help us or not?"

"Help you, how?" She opened her door and forced him to shuffle backward on the gravel.

"Oh, come on, Frankie," he said bitterly. "You know we're dying out here. And you've been on the inside of this story from the beginning. Give us a break."

"I'm a friend of the family," she answered coldly. "I don't know what you're talking about. But I'll tell you what I *will* do. When we come out I'll give you a *brief* rundown on where things stand as of now." She curled her mouth and added, "Here, let me tell the others—"

"No, wait," he replied quickly. "Why don't you just give *me* the rundown. The others'll pick up on it soon enough. I'll wait here by your car."

She sniffed and went around to the other side of the car, where Bishop Foster waited politely.

"Did you hear that?" she asked.

He nodded.

"Reporters would cut their own mothers' throats for a jump on the competition," she said. She grinned and added, "I would too. But it's pretty hard to get an exclusive with a weekly newspaper."

Blackie and Charlie met them on the porch, and Blackie pushed the doorbell. There was no immediate response, so he pushed it again, this time with a greater urgency.

"It's a big house, Chief Boone," Bishop Foster said quietly.

"And there aren't any servants," said Charlie. "Jake gave them an extra month off. With pay."

Though there was no sound of approaching footsteps, the door opened abruptly, and Winnie Taylor greeted them.

"So you're here," she said. "We've been expecting you. Please come in. It's quite a madhouse in here, but come in."

"A madhouse?" asked Blackie.

"Oh, we know all about the busted alibis. Jake's had ten calls from Longview—rats deserting the ship. And Uncle Jim called from the hospital . . . Mother's screwball confession."

"Do you know Bishop Foster?" Blackie asked, when they were in the foyer.

"We've met before," said the bishop warmly. "How are you, Miss Taylor?"

"Not bad," she replied. "Nice to see you again. Did you come to comfort us?"

"Not exactly. Actually, I'm the one who discovered your mother's confession—at St. Andrew's."

"Sounds sort of traitorous. Isn't that supposed to be covered by the secrecy of the confessional or something?"

"I'm afraid not."

Frankie asked, "Miss Taylor, did you know about your mother's confession?"

"Well, no."

"What I mean is, had your mother threatened to do this before?"

"Sure, if you put it that way. She was always talking about setting things right with God. That story about old man Erikson was no deep dark secret. Common family knowledge. Who knows if any of it's true—only Uncle Jim, I guess."

"Did your fiancé know about any of this?"

"Beaker, sure. Mother was always making cryptic references to it. Beaker pretended not to understand, but he knew. Jake and Greg and I talked it over with him—several times. We never thought she'd do it. She was all talk. But we wondered what the legal ramifications were. . . . I'm sorry to spoil your story, Mrs. Mills, but there's no mystery here."

"You may be mistaken," said Frankie softly.

While they were talking, Winnie Taylor had shepherded them down the marble hall toward the parlor.

They were met at the open door by Greg Taylor, who said without introduction, "I heard you were checking up on me in Tyler, Blackie. Satisfied?" His tone implied that his alibi at least—unlike his brother Jake's—was above reproach.

"Yes, satisfied," said Blackie.

Over Greg's shoulder, Frankie could see Edgar Brooks and Jake Taylor whispering agitatedly near the bar. Beaker Hogan stood relaxed to one side. The room itself was very bright. There was a large picture window that opened to the west, and the sun's long afternoon rays were reflecting off a dazzling variety of greens and yellows and reds.

When they were through the door, Edgar Brooks stepped forward to greet them. "Awful mess," he said nervously. "Stupid of us to try to cover up. My idea. Jake wanted to come clean from the beginning. . . . But the lady *is* married. His motive was old-fashioned gallantry."

"Very noble," said Frankie.

"Is everyone acquainted?" Blackie said, indicating Bishop Foster.

"Yes, no problem," answered the bishop. He smiled and nodded his greetings.

Charlie Swicegood took a position half inside and half outside the door, his thick black arms folded tightly against his chest.

Mayor Hogan said to Blackie, "Expecting trouble?"

Blackie laughed. "No, Beaker. Come on in, Charlie. No one's going to run."

Jake Taylor shook his head and said to Frankie, "Do you think the press'll make a big issue out of this . . . Mother's confession and this alibi business?"

Frankie nodded slowly. "I'm afraid so. They'll eat you alive."

"I may as well quit the Senate race right now."

"Who was this woman anyway, Jake?" Blackie asked.

"Does she have to be dragged into this?"

"No way to keep her out of it. What's her name?"

Jake gave it and then walked dejectedly back to the bar. After pouring himself another drink he called out, "She's a nice lady. Goddamn shame!"

"Will she verify your story?"

"Yes, no problem."

Edgar Brooks, who was perspiring heavily, said, "It was my fault. It was the Baptists I was worried about. You can't get caught with a married woman and get elected to the Senate. Not here."

Frankie addressed all three of Claudine's children. "Do you want to make a statement about your mother's confession?"

"Only that it was a lot of nonsense," Jake answered. "I don't know where she dreamed that stuff up. She must've got it in her mind years ago—kept building it up, adding to it, until it seemed like the truth. I'm sure she believed it. But I assure you, it's fantasy. Mother made it a practice to trot out that story every two or three years. But I'll admit I never thought she'd make it public. She was full of threats."

"When you think about it, she didn't make it public this time either," said Greg Taylor. "The bishop here found the confession—well hidden, I imagine."

Blackie said to Jake, "And James called you Saturday night to tell you your mother'd made another threat?"

"Yes. Mother told Karen Erikson the story . . . probably

complete with tears—I've seen those often enough—and
Karen ran straight to Uncle Jim."

"What was your reaction when you got James's call?"

"Concern naturally. I didn't believe she'd do anything, but
you never know. Uncle Jim and I hashed it over and agreed
that he should call Mother. She was always a little afraid of
him. . . . But he didn't kill her, if that's what you're thinking."

"Did you know there was a *written* confession?"

"Mother never said. But that's the impression I always
had."

"Why didn't you find it and destroy it years ago, if you
were so concerned? That shouldn't have been too difficult."

"What would that accomplish? She could've just written
another."

"Why do you think Claudine called Father Stickney Saturday night and gave him the document?"

"Probably because James was extra rough on her. We
agreed that that was the best approach. We were getting
tired of her threats."

Greg Taylor said, "If you ask me, I think Mother's intention was for Father Stickney to hide that confession for
another twenty-five years. From what Uncle Jim said on the
phone, the damn thing's been around since 1958. Hardly a
sense of urgency on Mother's part, eh? She liked being rich
and respected. But she wanted God's approval, too. Giving
the confession to the priest for safekeeping was probably as
far as she intended to go."

Edgar Brooks bit his lower lip and traced his jowls with
his thumb. The perspiration on his face and neck had grown
so heavy that he was no longer bothering to control it. He
stared blankly into his drink.

"Which will hurt us the most, Edgar?" said Jake. "This alibi
business or Mother's craziness?"

"The confession," he said, after a moment. "They'll play
up the genetics of the thing. Bad seed from a bad family. The
alibi—not as bad, but not good. I've already mentioned the
Baptists—"

"The politics will have to wait," said Blackie.

"It's all over anyway," said Edgar. "We'll *never* make it to the Senate now." He wheezed as he spoke and gulped for air.

Blackie said, "Jake, how long were you with this woman on Sunday?"

"From about eight till three-thirty or so. I got back to Edgar's just before you called to tell me about Mother. About four in the morning, wasn't it?"

"Where did you see her?"

"Her place."

"Where was her husband?"

"Houston—business."

Blackie jotted the information in his notebook and then said, "Jake, I don't need to remind you that you'd better be square with me this time. If any of this isn't right you're going to have more trouble than even you can handle."

During the interrogation, Bishop Foster had moved closer to Beaker Hogan, and when it was clear that Blackie had completed his questioning, the bishop said, "Mayor Hogan, I've had a very interesting discussion with Judge Susan Moreno."

Hogan laughed. "Oh, ho! That's a pretty transparent opening, isn't it, Padre? I suppose you're worried about the Church losing out. Too bad, Padre, but Judge Moreno was quite mistaken about Claudine's intentions."

Blackie picked up on the change of topics and said to Jake, "Did you have any inkling of a change in your mother's will?"

"No. But I never kept up with her. She was always grousing about it one way or the other."

"How about you, Greg?" asked Blackie.

Greg frowned. "Mother chirped and chirped. I never listened."

Winnie volunteered, "For someone so interested in the next world, Mother had an inordinate fondness for money. In my opinion the situation with the will was the same as the confession: brinkmanship. So far and no farther. She wanted God to have the money . . . but not really. Tease Him with it a bit, but keep it in the family. It got *very* tiresome after a while."

Bishop Foster smiled pleasantly and suggested, "Perhaps Claudine grew weary of the game as well, and finally made the decision to truly leave her money to the Church."

"If I didn't know better, Padre," said Beaker Hogan, "I'd say that you were calling me a liar . . . in your gentle, clerical way, of course."

"No, no," the bishop replied smoothly. "That was not my intent at all. The Church has no reason to doubt your word. You certainly don't seem like the kind of man who would deprive God of what is rightfully His. I was merely exploring—speaking in general terms."

"Let me assure you," said Beaker, "that I received *no* communication from Claudine regarding a change in her will. And let me add that I'm a Catholic. If it'll help you to relax, I'll swear to this on Holy Mother Church."

"That won't be necessary," said the bishop, his smile gone and his eyes cold.

The reporter from *The Houston Post* listened eagerly to the rundown Frankie had promised. He whistled as she mentioned Claudine Taylor's confession, but he reserved his most emphatic exclamation for the revelation that Jake Taylor had lied about his whereabouts Sunday night.

"Boy, damn! What was that woman's name again? Say, I think I've heard of her husband. Heavy machinery or something. Does he know yet?"

Frankie shook her head. "I don't think so."

"Yeah, well thanks. I got to run now. Thanks again."

"The sex angle," Frankie said cynically to Bishop Foster. "Talk about big black headlines!"

"Won't Chief Boone object to your giving out so much information?"

"It's got to come out," said Frankie. "And soon. Blackie knows that. They might as well get it right. Anyway, I don't care what the hell he thinks."

The bishop smiled. "You didn't hoard the news like you said. You shared it. Newspeople aren't so cold-blooded after all."

"Only because I knew it wouldn't keep until my rag gets out Monday. If I could've, I'd've backstabbed them all!"

"And besides," Frankie said in the car as they returned to town, "I didn't tell the *Post* everything."

The bishop turned to look at her. "You sounded pretty thorough to me. What did you leave out?"

"The name of the killer."

"James Lan Franco?"

"No, we were wrong about that."

"You've got another suspect in mind?"

"Yes."

"Well . . . ?" the bishop inquired eagerly, taking his eyes off the road.

"Not yet," she said. "I need to think it through some more—to see how all the parts fit. I don't want to be wrong."

"Do you think you might be?"

"No."

19

FRANKIE awoke Friday morning with paradoxical emotions. On the one hand she wished to postpone the fearsome revelations waiting at the Tyler Diagnostic Clinic; on the other she wished to face up to the truth as quickly as possible.

She gave in to the former and rolled over in bed. She pulled the blankets over the back of her neck and buried her face in the pillows. What would be the first indication of venomous news? The whispers behind the reception desk? The averted eyes of Dr. Ishikawa's nurse? The doctor's first comforting sentence? She decided on the last and tried to formulate it in her mind: "We must be thankful, Mrs. Mills, for the two extra years that your cystectomy has given you. . . ."; or "I know you're a strong woman, Mrs. Mills, so I'll give this to you straight. . . ."; or (and at this point she began to giggle semi-hysterically under the covers) "You're looking exceptionally well this morning, Mrs. Mills—however, looks can be deceiving. . . ."

She snorted and rose up on both elbows while continuing to giggle. She remembered the old story about the Army recruit who had been called to inspection, not knowing that his father had just been killed in a horrible accident. The drill sergeant whose task it was to inform the young man of the tragedy called the men to formation and then barked, "All of you whose fathers are still alive take one step forward!" When the unsuspecting recruit began to take his step, the sergeant raised his hand and snapped, "Not so fast there, Brown!"

Well, maybe Dr. Ishikawa would be more gentle, but the results would be the same. Dead is dead.

She swung her legs over the side of the bed and groped with her feet for her house slippers. She found them and padded into the bathroom to empty her appliance.

How strange, she thought, when she had drained her bag and had cleaned and examined her stoma; how strange the adaptability of the human race. A year and a half earlier, just the thought of living with an alien device clinging to her side was enough to make her gag. But her doctors in New York had told her that the initial revulsion would pass and that before long she would grow used to the excess baggage. And they had been right. Not only had she become accustomed to the inconvenience, but she had developed an almost motherly regard for the new additions to her body. It was true that she often neglected them because of the pressures of running a newspaper, but that did not mean that she did not appreciate them. She had even given them nicknames (which she had later heard was not uncommon). The round pink hole of her stoma she had called Todd, after her ex-husband (though she felt it would have been more appropriate if she had had rectal cancer instead of bladder cancer, since Todd was such an asshole). And the appliance itself she had named Mike, after her old boss at *The New York Times* (like Mike Winchester, the device was extremely demanding and needed constant attention). None of this was to say that the bladder removal and its aftermath was a pleasant experience. Certainly not. It was the most ghastly experience imaginable. Yet it was endurable.

And one problem surmounts another. The urostomy was no longer a major difficulty in her life. She could handle that. But could anyone handle cancer of the kidneys?

She shook her head and went into the kitchen to fix herself a cup of tea. The morning was already quite warm and she decided against a robe.

As she sat with her hands clasped around the steaming

cup, she reflected on how much she enjoyed being single. Her only responsibility was to herself. There was no over-bearing male stumbling about her bathroom, calling her away from this quiet moment with insistent requests. But of course she understood that because her marriage had been so cruelly unsuccessful, she was now soured on the whole institution. She knew there were happily married couples around. She had just never met any.

Sex was a problem. She missed it. Todd, for all his hypoc-risies, had been a superb lover—even though he always seemed to be performing rather than loving. Still, she chuckled, he was a damn good performer.

Blackie Boone would like to step in, she knew. But he was simply not her type. She had never been attracted to fleshy men. At first she had patronized him intellectually, but she now realized that he was every bit as smart as she, and prob-ably a whole lot smarter. But that didn't matter. It was a physical thing. She could never take him for a lover. And yet she found him to be a warm, concerned companion. She knew he understood how arrogant he had been in violating her privacy, and after a few more snubs on her part, he would understand it even better. And then perhaps they could examine the possibilities of friendship.

She smiled. Here she was again, planning for the future. A future that she had no right to consider.

Well, it was time to stop procrastinating and to face real-ity. She put her empty cup in the sink and went back to the bedroom to dress for her drive to Tyler.

She tried to maintain a single-minded attitude. It some-how seemed inappropriate to think of anything but the state of her health. But like the student of Latin on death row, she discovered that she still had other interests and that the overwhelming question could not occupy her entire mind.

She thought about the murders. She was virtually certain who had committed them, and why. The logic was inescap-able. She wondered if Blackie knew also. Maybe not. It was probably true that his mind was a little sharper than hers, but he didn't have twenty years of newspaper experience

behind him. The organizing, the shifting, the including and the excluding—these were the habits that had shown her the truth. Blackie may be able to peer more deeply into the heart of a mass of information than she, but he couldn't shape it as quickly or as effectively. And this was a case that required *shape*.

In the waiting room at the Tyler Diagnostic Clinic, she picked up a copy of *The Houston Post*. The headlines did not surprise her:

MURDER OLD AND NEW

And, in a slightly smaller type running across the top of the page:

CONGRESSMAN TAYLOR IN LOVE TRIANGLE

The *National Enquirer* would be proud, she thought.

The stories that followed each headline were straight from the information she had provided at Fairfield. She read the second lead first, as she knew most would. It carried the byline of her friend:

> Sources close to the Claudine Taylor murder in-
> vestigation in Kilkenny have reported that Con-
> gressman Jake Taylor, who is running for the
> United States Senate, has admitted that he lied to
> the police concerning his whereabouts last Sun-
> day night. He was actually in the company of a
> married Longview woman, Mrs. . . .

She hurriedly scanned the rest of the story, which told how the woman's husband, a wealthy manufacturer of earth-moving equipment, had scoffed at the entire matter—citing the vivid imaginations of bored reporters. The report then went on to tell how Jake Taylor was properly contrite over the situation, and how no one had accused him of any wrongdoing in the death of his mother.

The lead story, which was subtitled DEATH IN THE PINEY WOODS, also carried her friend's byline. She smiled. Not bad—a double byline on the front page. Can't ask for much more than that:

> The Taylor and Lan Franco fortunes, it was alleged today, were built on a foundation of blackmail, corruption, and death. The accuser was none other than Claudine Taylor herself, the recently murdered matriarch, whose posthumous confession was discovered among the effects of Father Robert Stickney. Stickney, it will be remembered, was himself brutally . . .

Frankie ran her eyes quickly over the remainder of the article, touching the high points to be sure her friend hadn't embellished the facts with his propensity for wretched excess. Apparently not. Everything seemed to be in order.

She was about to close the newspaper when two side bars caught her attention.

The first, which was presented inside a black-bordered box, read:

PRESIDENT SUPPORTS TAYLOR 1000 PERCENT

> The office of the President of the United States said today that the unfortunate events in Texas do not in any way alter the Chief Executive's support for Jake Taylor's election to the Senate. Both the Republican Party and the President personally stand squarely behind Congressman Taylor and look forward to his tenure in the highest legislative body in the land.

But at column-left bottom was a late bulletin that told a different story:

JAKE TAYLOR WITHDRAWS FROM SENATE RACE
See Section D

They ought to get together on these releases, Frankie thought. But she smiled at the mix-up. Watching politicians make asses of themselves was one of her favorite pastimes.

She fumbled through the paper looking for Section D, but before she could find it, Dr. Ishikawa's nurse appeared at the door and announced, "Frankie, the doctor will see you now."

The examination room seemed icy cold, and for a moment Frankie wondered why the hell they didn't turn down the air conditioning, but then she realized that the room's temperature was normal and the chill was in her blood.

She watched Norma go about her duties, and tried to determine from her appearance and her actions whether the death sentence was about to be decreed. But the busy nurse was unreadable. Her actions were neutral, her eyes were steady and calm, and her facial expressions were bland. If she knew anything she was a pro at keeping it to herself.

The door began to open and then stopped. Frankie could hear Dr. Ishikawa talking to someone in the hallway. His hand was still on the knob and it rotated slowly as if he couldn't decide whether to come in or stay out. Finally she could hear the other voice growing fainter as it moved down the hall, and Dr. Ishikawa entered the room.

God, she was nervous! Her hands shook, her neck trembled, and she could barely keep her eyes focused.

The diminutive internist walked straight toward her and put his hand on her arm.

Here it comes, she thought. That first comforting sentence. A positive followed by the inevitable tragic negative. They must study this somewhere in medical school: Breaking the Bad News 202. She tensed.

"Pyelonephritis," the young doctor said, smiling.

She looked up sharply. What the hell kind of first sentence was that? "I beg your pardon," she said.

"Pyelonephritis," he repeated. "I'm very pleased to tell you, Mrs. Mills, that you have no tumor, no additional malignancy. What you have is pyelonephritis."

She started, "Pyel—you mean I don't have kidney cancer? Is that what you're telling me?"

"Exactly."

"Well, I'll be . . ." She shot a look of triumph at Norma, who returned it with a huge grin. "No cancer, Norma," she called out giddily, hunching her shoulders and raising her palms upward.

"None," said the nurse.

Frankie's eyes filled with moisture and for several seconds she could say nothing at all. The doctor and the nurse waited patiently. Finally she wiped her tears on her sleeve and said, "I was so afraid. . . ."

"Who wouldn't be?" said Norma.

Dr. Ishikawa broke in, his face stern. "I'm delighted, Mrs. Mills, that our first estimate was wrong. . . . But the good news comes hand in hand with other problems. Pyelonephritis is not the common cold. It is quite serious in and of itself."

"What is it?" asked Frankie.

"Bacterial infection. But more . . . pyelitis that has spread to all portions of the kidneys. It can last many months or even years, all the while causing serious damage. I suspected it—the pain in the back, the fever, the cloudy urine. But with your history, a tumor was our first item of business."

"Have I damaged my kidneys?"

"We don't think so."

"Thank God."

"Don't be too proud of yourself, Mrs. Mills. The pyelitis was almost certainly your fault—not draining your appliance frequently enough, not keeping your stoma clean. You brought this all on yourself."

Frankie nodded submissively. "What can be done?" she asked.

"Pyelonephritis can be treated with sulfa compounds and antibiotics. I've mapped out a complete program for you. Also, we want to make absolutely certain that *nothing* is interfering with the normal flow of urine. It has to flow freely to stay clean. Bacteria love all stagnant pools."

"Will I be all right?" she said softly.

"I'll see to it," he answered with a smile.

20

EUPHORIA. How can a woman who has lost a major organ to a devastating malignancy feel euphoric over the state of her health? Easy, thought Frankie. On the steering wheel, she tapped a rhythmic accompaniment to the country-and-western tune blaring from her car radio. She pulled into her parking space in front of the *Kilkenny Weekly Times* and stepped exultantly onto the sidewalk.

The warm June sun increased her sense of well-being, and she waved merrily at two passing businessmen—both of whom turned to stare.

Inside the office, Gabe Sullivan greeted her with news that dampened her spirits. "James Lan Franco's taken a turn for the worse. He's not expected to live out the day."

She laid her purse on her desk and turned to face the printer. "Are they certain?"

"Absolutely. Blackie called. He'd just talked to Knox Presley. James's liver is leaking like a kitchen strainer. And listen to this: The old fool polished off a quart of Jack Daniels last night—right there in the hospital. Beta snuck it in to him. Like pouring gasoline down his throat."

Frankie nodded absently and sat down in her chair. Sullivan returned to the pressroom.

One life extended and one life shortened, she thought as she reached for the telephone. One lease renewed, one canceled. Who could understand it?

"St. Andrew's Chapel," the voice on the other end of the line said.

"Hello, Bishop Foster," she replied. "Francesca Mills. Want to have lunch?"

"I'd be delighted—but I can't. Seems that James Lan Franco's developed a sudden interest in religion—wants to discuss the eternal welfare of his soul. Frankly, I'd rather have lunch with you."

"And I thought I was cynical."

"What's up, Mrs. Mills?"

"Not a damn thing. I was just sitting here asking myself who in this town I'd like to spend the next hour with, and I decided it was you."

"I'm flattered."

"You should be. Will you be hearing James's confession?"

"Probably."

"Do people ever lie to their priests?"

"All the time."

"Even on their deathbeds?"

He laughed. "This is getting dangerously close to violating—"

"I'm just generalizing. I know you can't share what he tells you. I guess I'm just wondering if it'd be worth sharing."

She rejected a temptation to call Blackie and had lunch alone at the Ramada Inn. When she returned to the office, she sat at her desk and slipped a sheet of paper into her typewriter.

She had never had any difficulty getting started with her writing. To her it was a job, plain and simple. Inspiration was for misty-eyed poets and frustrated novelists. She began immediately:

MURDER AS REPORTED IN A

SMALL TOWN WEEKLY NEWSPAPER

By the time you read this, the hot news will be cold. All of the bulletins, all of the scoops, and all

of the exclusives relating to the Kilkenny murders
will have been sucked drier than a west Texas real
estate development. The big city papers and the
television and radio stations will have kept you informed about these killings on a daily (even
hourly) basis. By now you know every fact and
every name and every other detail associated with
these tragedies. (You believe.)

So what is a two-bit country weekly to do? Why
bother with this story at all? Why not give up and
let the big boys handle it?

The answer is simple. There's a lot more to tell.
A two-minute account by a white-toothed television commentator is not enough; a shallow article
by a byline-hungry reporter is not enough; even a
so-called in-depth study in the "Insight" section of
your newspaper is not enough—not when written
by an uninformed or a partially informed jour-
nalist.

This is a story that requires background and un-
derstanding and personal involvement. It is a story
of great poignancy and bitter irony; of broken
hearts and shattered lives; of betrayal, suicide, and
murder.

It is a story of the past and of the present.

It is a story of a golden-haired girl who stepped
off a train nearly fifty years ago with her dreams
and her hopes. . . .

Frankie continued to type for nearly three hours at more
than ninety words a minute. When she finally leaned back to
evaluate what she had written, her neck was sore and her
head ached; but she was satisfied. She knew she was on the
right track. She still had a long way to go—she hadn't even
begun the section on the present-day murders—but the
work was going smoothly and it was now just a matter of
time and discipline.

She put the finished pages in her top drawer and covered

the typewriter. The rest could wait. There were still two days left until the *Kilkenny Weekly Times* hit the street.

Before she could push away from the desk, the phone rang and she answered it gaily.

"I've been waiting for you to call," said Blackie Boone. "But I think your voice tells me what I wanted to know."

"You didn't call Tyler this time?" Frankie asked sarcastically.

"No."

"I'm fine, Blackie. Really fine. No cancer. False alarm."

There was a long pause on the other end of the line and finally he replied, "That's great. That kind of news is worth waiting for. . . . What's been the problem then?"

"Kidney infection—just like I said. But it's the truth this time. Serious and not to be taken lightly, but a whole lot better than I expected. Pyel—something."

"I'm happy for you, Frankie."

"I know you are, Blackie."

"Have you heard the news about James Lan Franco?"

"Yes, Gabe told me."

"A few more hours at the most. He looks like hell and he's sinking fast. With him gone we may never find out what's happened here. But I'm not giving up. I'm going to the hospital as soon as Bishop Foster finishes his business. He and James have been huddled all afternoon."

"Blackie, James couldn't tell you anything if he wanted to. At least not about the present-day murders. Sure he killed Samuel Erikson forty years ago, but we have to face the fact that he's gotten away with that—at least in this life—and if he straightens things out with Bishop Foster he figures on getting away with it in the next. But as far as his sister's death goes, or the priest's, he didn't have a damn thing to do with them—not directly anyway."

"You sound pretty sure of yourself."

"I am. It was like writing a news story. You line up your facts one by one and you tick them off as you include them in your article. Those that are extraneous to your central point you discard. When you're writing about a fire, you don't include the color of the fire chief's boots. Blackie, when I started to get this thing in shape in mv mind, including and excluding, I realized that some of the central facts fit some of the suspects, and some fit others, but all of them fit only one. I may have arrived at my conclusion backwards— by eliminating those who didn't fit—but I'm convinced the conclusion is sound."

"Who is it?" said Blackie firmly.

"When are you going back to the hospital?" she asked.

"In an hour or so. Five o'clock."

"I'll meet you there," she said, hanging up the phone.

21

I N the outer room of James Lan Franco's hospital suite, Frankie said to Edgar Brooks, "But why did you pull Jake out of the Senate race? The President and the party seemed to be behind you. One thousand percent, I believe the President said."

"Pure bullshit," he answered. "They made us quit. The party chairman called to make it clear they were out of it. If we tried to make it on our own, they wouldn't lift a finger to help us."

"What about the President?"

"He *is* the party. All that stuff in the newspapers about standing squarely behind us was crap to make it look like Republicans are loyal—united. If we tried to keep running we'd have to do it alone, and *nobody* gets elected alone—not to the United States Senate!" He spit out the last phrase in a childish, singsong voice, and Frankie realized that the sweaty little campaign manager had been drinking heavily.

"What are your plans now?" she asked.

"Mine—me personally? . . . Back to the House with Jake—until November at least. After that I guess I'll be back in Austin and Baton Rouge kissing up to semiliterate clowns from La Grange and Shreveport." He coughed and shook his head sadly.

Also in the room were Blackie Boone, Beta Lan Franco, and Jake, Winnie, and Greg Taylor.

Blackie put his arm around Beta, who was crying softly.

He turned her toward him and drew her to his chest. Her small, gray head bobbed up and down on his shoulder. "Go ahead, cry," he said gently. ". . . But that liquor, you shouldn't have—"

She raised her head and said, "I know. You've been telling me all day. It's just that James begged and begged. He kept saying, 'What's the difference? I'm dying anyway. Give me a little pleasure if you love me.' . . . I broke down."

Blackie nodded and held her tighter. "It's all right," he said quietly. "It's all right."

Dr. Knox Presley came through the open door, followed closely by Mayor Beaker Hogan.

Dr. Presley motioned toward the inner room. "What's going on in there?" he asked.

"The priest's still with him," said Winnie.

"Well, I've got to go in now," the doctor said officiously, "priest or no priest."

Winnie smirked. "His soul will just have to wait, is that it, Knox, while you keep his body alive a couple more hours?"

Beaker Hogan took a position next to Winnie, and slipped his arm around her waist. "Hell of a mess," he said, "this whole week."

Frankie asked, "What are your plans now, Beaker? Are you still going to run for Jake's House seat?"

"That depends on Jake," he replied. "If he decides to have another go at the House, I'll step aside."

"Jake's all washed up," Edgar Brooks said coldly. "We *all* are. You'd better take a closer look at your situation, Beaker. You're tied in pretty close to the Taylors—family lawyer . . . marrying Winnie. Tainted family, tainted candidates. You'll be getting your call from the party real soon now." He laughed and walked heavily toward the couch on the far side of the room.

Blackie came up beside Frankie and whispered, "When are you going to tell me what's on your mind? I might be able to help, you know."

She frowned and turned to face him. "Oh, Blackie," she said softly, "you've done ninety percent of the detective work on this case. I don't mean to act like I'm some kind of Sherlock Holmes. You've laid the groundwork for everything. . . . Might be able to help? You've done it all." She looked around to see if anyone could hear, and then she said, "Of course I'll tell you. It's just the logical result—the shape of all your work. You'll see what I mean quickly enough."

But before she could continue, the inner door opened and Bishop Foster exited the bedroom.

Dr. Presley, who had not carried through with his threat to interrupt the religious encounter, said huffily, "It's about time. The man needs medical attention." He headed toward the door.

"Not anymore." said Bishop Foster, a dark red color about the rims of his eyes. "He just died."

Dr. Presley brushed past the bishop on a dead run and disappeared into the oilman's room. Beta Lan Franco screeched and raced after him. No one spoke for what seemed to Frankie to be five or ten minutes but what she knew was closer to one or two. Then the doctor came out very slowly, nodding his head. Beta could be heard in the next room alternately crying and screaming and begging her husband not to leave her.

Dr. Presley shut the door behind him. "She wants to be alone. . . . There's no hope, no pulse, no life at all. We could get the whole staff in here—it wouldn't help." He sank down on the couch next to Edgar Brooks.

The room was silent for a few more moments, and finally Jake Taylor, who looked tired and subdued, said, "Blackie, has Mother's body come back from Dallas yet?"

"Yes, she's at Marsh's. All three of the bodies—your mother's, Karen Erikson's, and Father Stickney's—were brought back this morning."

"Well, we've got another one now," said Greg Taylor, pointing toward the closed door. "I don't suppose you'll need an autopsy on Uncle Jim, will you?"

"No," said Blackie. "Knox'll just sign a death certificate."

"We need to get busy on Mother's funeral," said Jake.

"And it looks like we'd better do something about Uncle Jim's, too. Aunt Beta's not going to be in any kind of condition to handle it."

Bishop Foster said, "I'll be glad to handle your mother's requiem. I'm doing James's—at his request."

"That'd be fine," said Jake. "I'll call Roy Griddle at Marsh's and have him get started on the arrangements."

Greg moved closer to Bishop Foster and said with a sneer, "Did Uncle Jim break down . . . cry and moan and all that stuff? Beg God's forgiveness? I'll say this for him, he always played all the angles."

Bishop Foster ignored him, but Greg went on. "What about Mom? Did he kill her . . . and that nutty priest? Don't people have to confess all their sins to get into this heaven of yours? And what about all that old stuff that Mom whined about in her confession? Was it true? He couldn't leave that out, could he? God knows everything . . . the all-seeing eye. If poor old Uncle Jim skipped anything he'd burn in purgatory, right?"

"Shut up, Greg!" said Winnie.

Bishop Foster stared contemptuously at the young man and then walked toward Blackie and Frankie.

But Greg called after him, "John Lennon had it right, didn't he, when he wrote about heaven and hell. . . . That's why you murdered him, isn't it?"

Bishop Foster, a puzzled look on his face, turned back toward Greg. "I beg your pardon?" he said.

Frankie said, "He's talking about John Lennon's murder, Father. . . . Some sort of collective guilt from the religious establishment."

"Oh, I see."

Jake walked swiftly to his brother and grabbed him by the collar. "Shut your goddamn mouth, you stupid fool!" And with one quick thrust he backed him into the wall, where he released him. Even though Greg was younger and more powerful, he gave no resistance and continued to lean against the wall with a derisive grin on his face.

Bishop Foster said to Frankie, "How are you, darling?"

She took both of his hands and replied energetically, "I'm wonderful. . . . And I'm going to be getting better."

He smiled and patted her hand. "I'm so very glad," he said. "I have to admit I thought about you more than I should have this afternoon." He nodded toward James's room. "I tried to give him my complete attention, but I'm only human."

Blackie asked, "Is there anything at all you can tell us about what went on in there this afternoon?"

"I'm afraid not."

"It might've helped, that's all," Blackie mused. "I'm really not trying to pry. I just thought there might've been something that's not covered by these secrecy vows—some hint or something."

Bishop Foster did not respond.

Frankie said, "I'm halfway through my story for Monday's paper. James might've helped with the part I've already written—the murder of Samuel Erikson—but he wouldn't have been able to add anything to the second half."

"What's the second half?" Blackie asked.

"The murders of Claudine Taylor and Father Stickney, and the naming of their killer."

"Can you write that half?" asked the bishop.

"Yes."

The three Taylors and Beaker Hogan had picked up on the conversation and had begun to close in on the spot where Blackie, Frankie, and the bishop stood. Edgar Brooks and Knox Presley had risen from the couch and were now positioned slightly behind Bishop Foster.

"What're you saying, Mrs. Mills?" asked Winnie.

"That when my story is finished—and it's now just a matter of getting the words on paper—there'll be no unanswered questions about our present-day deaths. As far as what happened forty years ago—I'm afraid that mystery died with James Lan Franco." She looked straight into Bishop Foster's eyes as she spoke, to make it clear that she knew the possibility existed that *he* knew the truth.

"Well, tell us your story then," said Jake skeptically. "Let's see what you think you know."

"By all means," Winnie agreed.

Frankie looked at Blackie, who indicated with a slight nod that she should go ahead.

She was now in the center of a rough circle that had formed as the discussion progressed. She took a deep breath, wondering what she had gotten herself into, and said, "Fine, I'd be happy to."

22

"WHY don't we skip the part of the story I've already written," she said slowly, "and concentrate on what's to come? If you're interested in the first half, you can read it Monday. I believe I'll begin the second half with Karen Erikson's arrival in Kilkenny on Friday night. . . . She's lived a life of dissipation on various skid rows around the country, and now she's decided to come home. Why? Hard to say. Probably she's tired of living and wants to end it all here in East Texas. Maybe she's not consciously thinking of suicide yet, but the notion's somewhere in the back of her mind."

"I thought you were talking about murder, not suicide," said Edgar Brooks scornfully. "Where does the old lady fit into it?"

"Please give me a chance to tell my story," she replied politely. "On Saturday morning, Karen Erikson and Claudine Taylor unexpectedly meet somewhere downtown, and Claudine invites Karen to come to Fairfield later that afternoon. Claudine has been building up guilt for forty years, and one can only speculate what the sight of Karen has done to her. . . . Karen spends early Saturday afternoon with Bridie Embry—her old schoolteacher—and then goes out to Fairfield, where Claudine reveals the truth about Samuel Erikson's murder. She also informs Karen that at long last she plans to confess to the crime."

"Now wait a minute," Jake cut in, "you'd better not write

it that way. There's no evidence that any of Mother's old fantasies are—"

"Excuse me. I should have said, Karen hears Claudine's *version* of those events of forty years ago. Whether that version stemmed from hysterics or from reality, we'll never know, but nevertheless, that's what Karen heard. . . . She then leaves Fairfield and heads for James Lan Franco's mansion to confront her old lover—if such was actually the case—with these revelations."

Jake Taylor frowned at Frankie's obviously cynical attempt to placate him.

She went on. "James was either indignant over his sister's daydreams or concerned that the truth would finally come out—depending on your point of view—and so he gets on the phone with Jake to discuss the best way to handle her. But, of course, one of the keys to this whole matter is that this is nothing new—irritating, to be sure—but not new. Claudine has made such threats before . . . often.

"Karen, in the meantime, goes back to the Ramada Inn, where on Sunday morning she takes several healthy swallows of carbolic acid. Exit Karen Erikson.

"At this point in my story I intend to introduce the killer, not by name as yet—although by Monday his name will be known all over the country—but by motive. I suppose it's silly not to identify someone whom everyone reading my story already knows, but suspense is suspense, and even retrospective suspense gets 'em. Do we ever tire of reading *Murder on the Orient Express,* even though we've known for years that they *all* did it?

". . . The killer's motive was fear—to be very general. I thought originally that it might be greed, and that Claudine Taylor's will might be at the heart of it." She cast a quick glance at Beaker Hogan and Winnie Taylor, both of whom remained impassive. "But I rejected that idea when it became clear that Father Stickney's murder would be superfluous if that were the case. No, the motive was fear all right—and to be specific, fear of Claudine Taylor's confession."

"Get to the point," said Jake, his voice impatient.

Blackie nodded. "Please, Frankie," he said.

She said, "Then let's go straight to Sunday night. . . . After a day spent fretting and fussing, the murderer resolves to kill Claudine and end the threat once and for all. But, as in most hastily planned crimes, he leaves a trail of mistakes—all of which Blackie and his men uncover virtually at once." She turned toward Blackie and smiled.

"He?" said Bishop Foster.

"Yes. I'll begin to use the masculine pronoun now, since it's obvious that a woman, except as an accomplice, couldn't have managed these very physical murders."

"What mistakes are you talking about?" asked Dr. Presley.

"For one thing," she replied, "he forgets to break open a window or jimmy open a door, really a very stupid blunder since his intention is to make it appear that a transient is responsible. And with no sign of forced entry, the police deduce immediately that he has a key."

"Not a very important clue," said Beaker.

"Not by itself, but look at his other mistakes. He figures—incorrectly—that the confession is in her safe, so he comes prepared with the combination written on a small slip of paper. But remember, his plan is to cast the blame on a burglar, so after he breaks Claudine's neck he stabs her in both shoulders to make it appear that the combination was tortured out of her. He then leaves the slip of paper on top of the open safe. But the writing is too neat, too precise. No burglar would take such care in such a situation, a mistake that leads the police to another conclusion: He has a *right* to the combination.

"His third mistake is the manner in which he pulls off the road to allow Charlie Swicegood to pass by on his way to answer Claudine's call for help. Only a man familiar with those roads would know about that hidden turnoff.

"The next morning he continues his string of mistakes. He figures—correctly this time—that Claudine has given the confession to Father Stickney for safekeeping. But he under-estimates the blasting power of a shotgun at close range.

When he uses his weapon to torture his victim to discover the whereabouts of the confession, he miscalculates and ends Stickney's life. Not a very clever killer, eh? But of course he would've killed the priest in any case. He could've identified him.

"But his greatest mistake is in resolving to commit the murders in the first place."

"You're not going to give us a moralistic lecture on the evils of murder, are you?" said Greg.

"No indeed," said Frankie. "His greatest mistake is not in his resolution to kill other human beings—that mystery is beyond me—but in *believing it necessary* to make such a resolution."

"Sounds like a fine line to me," said Edgar Brooks, almost too softly.

"Not so fine. . . . You see, there was really no necessity to commit murder, no urgency to stop Claudine Taylor from making her confession public. She had stopped herself— over and over again—for twenty-five years, and longer. It was likely she would do so again. She was a nuisance, a bother, but not a genuine threat. Everyone who was a suspect in this case knew that . . . everyone but you, Edgar."

"Me!" the squat politician exclaimed. "What're you saying?"

"I'm saying that you killed Claudine Taylor and Father Robert Stickney."

Jake Taylor shook his head. "That's the stupidest thing I've ever heard."

Edgar stepped closer to Frankie, thrust his face forward, and said pugnaciously, "You'd better not say that in your newspaper. I'll sue your ass right out of—"

Blackie started to intervene, but Frankie restrained him with an upraised palm. She turned to Jake Taylor. "Think about it, Jake," she said. "After James called you Saturday night, did you tell Edgar about the conversation?"

"Of course. He was sitting right there."

"What was his reaction?"

"He was concerned, just like I was."

"Did you tell him that your mother had made these threats before—many times?"

". . . Well, no."

"What was his attitude for the rest of that night . . . and Sunday?"

"He was upset, of course. He talked about what Mother's confession would do to my Senate chances. . . . But I talked about it, too."

"Who kept bringing up the subject?"

"Well, he did."

"How many times?"

"Now that you mention it, a number of times. I got a little tired of it after a while." He looked strangely at Edgar.

"Again I ask you to think about it, Jake," said Frankie. "On Saturday night you presented your campaign manager with a problem that seemed, to him at least, insolvable. He had no way of knowing it was a false crisis. You neglected to tell him about your mother's past history. Everyone in the family knew all about Claudine's old story regarding the Eriksons. Everyone except Beta Lan Franco, perhaps. But can you really picture that little old woman breaking Claudine's neck? No. Then that leaves Edgar Brooks. He had the means, the overwhelming motive—if you fail, he fails—and the opportunity."

Jake Taylor turned to his advisor. "Edgar . . ."

Frankie added, "He certainly had the means. In your papers and personal effects, he had the combination of the safe and the keys to Fairfield, and he'd been out there often enough to know about that little side road. And he's a heavy, powerful man who owns guns and knives." She paused, rubbed her eyes with her fingers, and began again. "Concerning his opportunity, the one thing we all overlooked was that the alibis he concocted protected him as well as you. Where was *he* Sunday night, Jake, when you were with your lady friend?"

The congressman shrugged to indicate that he didn't know.

"And early Monday morning," Frankie went on, "after you

took him to his house in Longview, wasn't there plenty of time for him to grab his shotgun and sneak back to St. Andrew's Chapel?"

Edgar said, sniffing, "You have no proof—"

Blackie cut in, "I'm sure we could check his guns to see which has been fired recently. Dallas can check the spray patterns of the shot and—"

"No, I don't think so, Blackie," said Frankie. "That gun's at the bottom of the Sabine or buried somewhere. He made a lot of mistakes, but he wouldn't be dumb enough to take the shotgun back home with him. . . . But let me ask Jake a question. How many shotguns does Edgar own?"

"Three—no, four. And rifles and pistols."

"Do you know his shotguns?"

"Yes."

"Well, then. You'll be able to tell if one is missing, right?"

"Yes." The color in the congressman's face had risen and his eyes had narrowed.

Greg said to Edgar, "So *you* killed Mother. *Politicians!*" He hissed the last word and it was obvious he was including his older brother in the condemnation.

Frankie continued to address Jake. "Remember in Blackie's office that first morning? How your mother's religion came up? You and Greg were going back and forth about it. I'm sure that's what started Edgar thinking about Father Stickney and St. Andrew's Chapel."

Jake nodded. "I remember," he said. "And I remember something else. On the way back to Longview he kept pumping me about Mother's relationship with the priest. Were they close? How close? Seemed innocent at the time. . . . And he kept asking me about Uncle Jim's second phone call Saturday night."

"James called you twice?"

"Yeah, right. The first time to talk about how to handle Mother. The second time to tell me how it went."

"Hadn't you discussed the second call with Edgar?"

"Yeah, sure. We'd talked about it. But I hadn't told him everything. It hadn't seemed important."

"And on the drive back to Longview Monday morning?"

"I told him everything I could remember. He kept harping on it, dragging it out of me. But he made it sound kind of natural. Mother dead, her priest, her religion and all. I told him how Uncle Jim had said that after he'd put the fear of God in her, she'd mentioned Father Stickney. Something to the effect that she wasn't alone—she did have someone to turn to."

"Good God," said Bishop Foster.

Frankie asked, "During that drive back to Longview, did he talk about the confession at all?"

"No, I don't think so."

"Doesn't that strike you as peculiar? For a day and a half he constantly harps about the harm such a document can do to the campaign, and now that your mother's dead, he doesn't mention it at all. He just probes you about Father Stickney."

Jake turned to Edgar and grabbed him violently by the collar. "You goddamned little son of a bitch!"

"No, Jake, please!" Edgar squealed.

"You did it, didn't you?" the irate congressman shouted as he tightened his grip.

Blackie Boone and Bishop Foster leapt forward simultaneously to restrain Jake, but not before Edgar cried, "Jake, I had to! . . . I thought I had to. Why didn't you tell me she'd said all that before? I couldn't see any other way. . . ." He lowered his head. "I couldn't stand the thought of going back to Austin and Baton Rouge."

"I don't think you'll have to worry about that," said Frankie.

23

THE following Thursday evening, Blackie, Frankie, and Bishop Foster sat at a prominent table in Will Stone's Sportsman's Paradise in Longview. They had just finished the most elaborate meal any of them had ever experienced: roast wild duck smothered in onions, apples and carrots, and secondary servings of venison chops, roast pheasant, and grilled redfish. Half-eaten and untouched side dishes of every conceivable vegetable were scattered around the table. All of this had been preceded by multiple cocktails and dozens and dozens of raw oysters with red sauce. The trio was happily surfeited and now watched contentedly while the proprietor himself poured brandy into huge snifters.

When Will Stone had heard that the false alibis he provided had been used to cover up a murder, he was humiliated. He had thought he was merely participating in the "good old boy" network and had no idea that he was being played for a fool. He was desperate to make things right. He insisted that Blackie Boone accept a complimentary dinner by way of apology. Blackie refused, but Stone would not take no for an answer. He pressed his invitation until the police chief finally relented—on the condition that two of his friends come along, too.

Frankie took a long, slow swallow of brandy and let the warmth spread. She felt superb. She had experienced a few episodes of severe pain during the past week, and they were

distinctly unpleasant, but she knew now what she was dealing with, and she could handle it.

She looked across the table at her two companions, who
were involved in an animated conversation . . . something to
do with heredity versus environment. Blackie was expound-
ing some theory or other about bad seeds, punctuating his
points with staccato pings on his brandy glass with his
thumb and forefinger; and Bishop Foster was responding
with pings of his own, while sternly pointing out that the
term *bad seeds* applied more to apple trees than to human
beings.

She was delighted with the evening, and delighted with
her new friends. Bishop Foster was a positive joy. Every new
day spent in his company brought new revelations of his
good nature and his gracious spirit. And Blackie, for his part,
was coming around fine. He had dropped completely his romantic allusions, and had begun to treat her in the same
manner that he did the bishop: respectfully, brotherly,
warmly.

"Oh, you ought to spend a little time in police work," said
Blackie to Bishop Foster. "You wouldn't be so damned lib-
eral if you did. You'd see people for what they really are."

The bishop chuckled. "Oh, I know what they *are*, Chief
Boone, believe me. Thirty years in the confessional has left
me with no doubts in that regard. But I prefer to concern
myself with what they can *become*."

Blackie shook his head and said to Frankie, "Set this guy
straight, would you? He's living in a dream world."

She smiled. "I like him just like he is," she said, raising her
snifter for another drink of brandy.

"Thank you, dear," Bishop Foster said. "By the way, I
meant to tell you how much I enjoyed your account of the
murders in Monday's paper. It was by far the best story I've
seen. I found myself in tears over Karen Erikson's wasted
life; and I must say that you treated everyone—even poor
Edgar Brooks—with a degree of sympathy."

"I'm changing," she said quietly. "I don't think I could've
written that story a year ago. I'd've spoiled it with black-and-

white judgments and smart-ass comments. I'm just beginning to understand, at my ripe old age, that we're all in this
together."

"Are you going to write any follow-up stories?" the bishop
asked.

"It's kind of hard to do that with a weekly newspaper. The
news gets stale real fast. But I may be able to do something
more with the personalities involved. Local stuff, of course.
Now that both Jake and Beaker have been pushed out of
national politics, there won't be much interest outside of
Gregg County."

"I saw where the President expressed deep regrets at
their withdrawals," said Blackie.

Frankie laughed. "Deep something, I'm sure, but hardly
regrets. It was all his idea."

"What do you suppose Mayor Hogan will do now?" the
bishop asked. "I can't see him continuing in local politics
after a taste—however brief—of the big time."

"Whatever he does," said Blackie, "he'll have plenty of
Taylor money to do it with. He found himself a gold mine in
Winnie. I've heard that each of the kids will get nearly ten
million."

Frankie chuckled. "He may need every dime to keep track
of his wife. Yesterday I saw her in an intimate little tête-à-
tête with a guy I know from *The Houston Post,* and I don't
think they were planning the Kilkenny Fourth of July pic-
nic."

Both men laughed, and Blackie said, "Poor Beaker. It
tends to even out, doesn't it?"

"What'll happen to Edgar Brooks, I wonder?" said Bishop
Foster.

"They're going for the death penalty," Blackie answered.
"Jake's running around saying how he wants to squeeze the
syringe himself. If you ask me, I think our congressman's lost
it—if he ever had it. Thirty years from now he'll be sitting
out at Fairfield, a bitter old man with his nose in a bottle."

"Greg's riding high," said Frankie. "I think I saw him on
TV with thirty or forty of his cohorts. They were demon-

strating in front of the White House—pouring chicken blood on an effigy of the President."

"How's Beta Lan Franco holding up?" asked Bishop Foster.

"Real well," Blackie replied. "She mourned for about two days, and then she snapped right out of it. I noticed today that she had a bunch of workmen out at Lan Franco Villa replacing that huge front door."

Frankie excused herself and went to the women's lounge to attend to her needs. While she was administering the necessary cleansing, the thought struck her that all over the world, thousands and perhaps hundreds of thousands of similarly handicapped individuals were performing the same ritual. When she was through, she did not immediately return to the dining room. In the front portion of the lounge, she found an overstuffed chair and made herself comfortable. After a few moments, she took a notebook from her purse and began to write down the positives and negatives of an idea that had begun to form in her mind. When she got up ten minutes later, she knew what she had to do when she got back to Kilkenny.

Epilogue

I N April of next year the Associated Press ran the following story:

PULITZER PRIZES AWARDED

New York (AP)—Columbia University announced the winners today in the sixty-ninth competition for journalism's most prestigious honors:

Spot News Photography—Timothy Branch of *The New York Times* for his daring series of photos from Warsaw as Soviet tanks moved in to close the city.

Distinguished Public Service—*The New York Times* for its reporting on local election fraud on the eastern seaboard.

Feature Photography—William Larson of the *Los Angeles Times* for photos from the California floods.

Literature—*Washington Post* reporter, David Allen Quentin, for his biography of Italian physicist, Enrico Fermi.

Local Reporting—Francesca Mills of the Kilkenny, Texas, *Weekly Times* for her sensitive reporting of the Kilkenny, Texas, murders.

Feature Writing—Francesca Mills of the Kilkenny, Texas, *Weekly Times* for her twelve-part series on her life as an ostomate.

Other newspapers and other awards included . . .